About the Author

Claire Boston fell in love with romance and romantic suspense at eleven when she discovered her mother's stash of Nora Roberts novels. Like Nora, she writes series set around families or groups of friends with a guaranteed happy ending.

She loves travelling and learning about new cultures and interesting vocations which she then weaves into her writing.

When Claire's not at the computer typing her stories she can be found dabbling in crafts, or curled up on the couch immersed in a book.

Claire lives in Western Australia with her husband, who loves even her most annoying quirks and is currently learning how to knit.

You can find her complete book list on her website https://claireboston.com/pages/reading-order.

You can connect with Claire through her Substack community.

http://www.claireboston.com/pages/reader-group/.

Also by Claire Boston

Romance
The Texan Quartet (4 books)
The Flanagan Sisters (4 books and a short story)
Love Me Do (Christmas Romance)

Romantic Suspense
The Blackbridge Series (8 books)
Retribution Bay (8 books)

Squadron 6
Rescuing Mila
Protecting Zoe

Lilydale Cottage
Repairing Dreams

Non-fiction
The Beginner Writer's Toolkit
Self-Editing

Protecting Zoe

Squadron 6

Claire Boston

BANTILLY
PUBLISHING

Protecting Zoe: Squadron 6

EPUB format: 9781922916198
Print: 9781922916204
Large Print: 9781922916211

Cover design by EmCat Designs
Edited by Ann Harth
Proofread by Teena Raffa-Mulligan

Chapter 1

Zoe Yelton glanced around the uncommonly quiet streets, and her skin prickled. Those on the Al Corniche were either a few tourists who had ignored the warnings to stay inside, or locals hurrying to get home.

The midday sun beat down relentlessly, and the palm trees lining the area gave little shade and almost nowhere to hide should something happen. She was out in the open, unprotected, in view of anyone.

Zoe placed a hand on her stomach to calm the nerves inside. She shouldn't be here. She had explicit instructions to pack her office and wait for the extraction team. But just after Zoe had arrived at the embassy with her suitcase, Nisha had called.

Zoe hadn't been able to ignore the desperation in Nisha's voice, despite her security training telling her that was exactly what she should do, so she'd offered to get everyone lunch and taken a bus to her destination. Thinking she knew better, just like she had that day in Coober Pedy.

No, this wasn't the same. She was an adult now and understood the risks. She rubbed the goosebumps on her arms.

Tension hung in the air, as dangerous as a gas leak waiting for a single spark.

In the distance, about two kilometres away, was the Tornado Tower building where the embassy was located. Where she should be right now. In the other direction were the main government buildings where the protests were rumoured to be taking place.

She was caught right in the middle.

Hurried footsteps made her whirl to face the small Pakistani woman who had begged her to come.

"Thank you for meeting me, Zoe," Nisha said, grabbing her arm, her grip strong.

"What's this about, Nisha? I shouldn't be here."

Nisha nodded. "People are already gathering at the meeting points. We have the support of many Qataris. We will win our rights."

Zoe hoped she was right, and perhaps the migrant workers had the numbers, but the Qatar government had military forces and, from the few skirmishes which had occurred over the past two weeks, they weren't afraid to use it. "Nisha, why do you need me?"

"We have proof." She drew out her phone and tapped frantically on the screen. "You need to help us save them."

Zoe frowned. "Save who from what?"

"Children from being taken by traffickers." Nisha thrust the phone at her. A zoomed in photo of several children getting into a van. The next photo those same children getting out at the container port, their expressions worried.

Zoe sucked in a sharp breath.

Nisha had told her about the children who were promised a better life in nearby countries only to be never heard from again. Zoe had said she'd help if she could, but she hadn't expected to be fleeing from civil unrest.

More photos of the six children being forced into a large, grey container, and she zoomed into one girl wearing a black hijab, whose eyes were wide as she looked for help. "Is that Maryam?"

Nisha nodded. "My cousin trusted the man who took her. Thought he was one of the honest ones."

Zoe had met Maryam at a gathering at Nisha's house. She'd been so excited about getting to wear the hijab now she'd reached puberty. They'd spoken in English while they'd prepared lunch together, and Maryam had been nothing but sweet innocence. Her gut clenched. "When were these taken?"

"Just now. The container is being loaded onto a ship."

"Who took them?" She handed the phone back to Nisha.

"My son. He works at the port. The ship is leaving today."

The entire city was about to erupt into chaos as the majority of migrant workers demanded more rights and fairer treatment. There was no way she could intervene today, not when she was due at the airport in less than an hour. "Nisha, I'm sorry. There's nothing I can do."

"Tell your government. They can send people."

Zoe shook her head. "It doesn't work like that." The embassy staff were being extracted before the riots started.

"There must be something you can do." Her voice trembled. "Maryam won't cope." The pain in Nisha's voice was impossible to ignore.

The chance at a better life for your child would be a hard one to resist. Over the year Zoe had been in Qatar she'd got to know the Pakistani migrant community. Nisha had been assigned as her cleaner, but Zoe hadn't needed help keeping her small apartment clean, so they'd spent the time talking, working on both Nisha's English and trying to improve their Arabic as well.

On Fridays she sometimes travelled to the Asian City to spend time with Nisha and the community she had built with the other Pakistani migrants in the country.

"I'll make some calls," Zoe promised. It sounded empty in her ears. She'd already raised the situation with Stefan when she'd first heard about it, but her boss had told her it wasn't their jurisdiction. The few contacts she had in Qatar hadn't been interested either.

What could she do in the time before she flew to the safety of Australia?

Not a hell of a lot. Frustration filled her. Those children thought they were helping their parents by leaving them to earn good money in decent jobs. Someone had to help.

Several buses drove by, noticeable by their shabbiness in a city full of high-end expensive vehicles. Inside were migrant workers, packed together heading for the government buildings.

Nisha glanced over. "It has started."

The words sent a deep frisson of fear through Zoe. She had to get back. "They *are* marching on Amiri Diwan?"

"Yes."

The government building was visible from the lookout point where they stood on Doha Bay. The streets were filling with more people, migrants rather than locals, and several of the tourists had finally noticed and started heading back to their accommodation.

"We don't have a lot of time. The ships may be delayed because there are no workers at the port," Nisha continued.

Which would have been advantageous if Zoe wasn't flying out of the country. But she couldn't tell Nisha that.

Nor could she leave without helping.

She glanced towards Tornado Tower, its sleek, shiny windows bright on the city skyline. Protestors were coming from that direction as well, as if all workers in the city had downed tools and were heading this way.

The streets were blocked, which meant she'd have to go on foot to get back to the embassy.

She was running out of time.

No one had expected the political situation to suddenly worsen, or for the embassy to decide to close its doors and return to Australia.

As if on cue, her phone rang, the noise shocking her, and she fumbled to turn down the volume as a few people turned their way.

Her boss.

She had to answer. "Hi, Stefan."

"Why the hell are you on the Al Corniche?" he bellowed. "You were supposed to be getting lunch."

Shit. She'd forgotten she had a GPS tracker on her phone. One of the security features of working overseas. "Saying goodbye to some friends."

"Well get your arse here. You should be helping us pack up the office. The extraction team will arrive in fifteen minutes."

And it would take her that long to walk the couple of kilometres to the embassy. It would be tight. At least the embassy was in the opposite direction to where the protestors were headed. "I'll be right there."

She hung up as an idea formed. "Send the photos to my email address." She handed Nisha a business card. "Can your son get close to the container?" Zoe asked, switching her phone to silent.

Nisha nodded.

Zoe hesitated only a second before handing Nisha her phone. "Give this to him. It has a GPS tracker on it. Tell him to get it to the children." She'd be back at the embassy for the extraction. She could get a new phone in Australia. "The code is two eight five three. Tell them to turn it off to conserve battery if I don't get them out before it sets sail." She had no idea how she would even do that. But she could figure out where the ship was making port and maybe free them when they arrived at their destination. "I have to go."

Nisha nodded. "Thank you."

She hugged her friend and then set off at a fast jog towards the embassy.

The call to prayer rang out across the city; the sound beautiful but haunting in the tense atmosphere.

As she jogged, two military trucks turned onto the main road which ran parallel to the Al Corniche, and several police vehicles followed protestors' cars along the road.

Zoe pushed herself harder, wishing she'd taken up jogging years ago. Her breath came in gasps, and her loose clothing flapped around her arms and legs as she ran. Sweat ran down her back as her head pounded from the heat.

Could she convince Stefan to help six innocent children being forced into slavery?

He always did things by the book. He'd tell her they didn't have the time to help a few children, that it wasn't their responsibility.

But there had to be some way she could save them.

No child, no person, should have to be at another person's whim. The migrants who travelled to the Middle East were after work and better lives for their families. It was how the traffickers got to them, with promises of good, high-paying jobs. Then they stole their passports and forced them to work for little or no pay.

The young boys were put to work as camel jockeys to allow rich locals to bet on camel races, and the girls, if they were lucky, became servants in someone's mansion.

Zoe's throat was dry as she reached the street the tower was on. She darted across the dual-carriageway and kept her gaze on the round building at the end of the street.

There was no sign the extraction convoy had arrived to pick them up, but without her phone she wasn't sure how much time had passed. Even if they had arrived, they might have pulled into the underground parking, which was off the street and potentially safer.

Behind her, the marching cry of the protestors began.

She was out of time.

***

Heath Ghanooni was looking forward to an easy mission for a change. The past couple had been hard with teammates getting injured and the one in Iran... well, it didn't bear thinking about. Helping an embassy team board a plane should be a piece of cake, as long as they got out before things kicked off.

The plane jolted as it hit turbulence, and he winced, trying not to be superstitious. He hadn't said the words aloud, but if he had, one of his teammates would have shoved him for jinxing the mission.

"Joker, you got anything else to add?" Dobby, his team leader, asked.

Heath glanced at the screen where they'd been planning for every eventuality. "One of the embassy staff might not want to leave," he said. "Or might decide they need to pack more information before they go, putting us behind schedule."

Radar nodded, his man bun bouncing. "Bound to be one idiot who doesn't understand the urgency of the situation."

"They've all been informed we're coming, right?" Axle asked, his preppy blond looks belying his lethality.

"Yeah, and they've been told to be at the embassy at thirteen hundred," Dobby confirmed. "So what's the plan with this douchebag?"

Heath grinned at the resignation in Dobby's voice. "Carry them out?"

"It can't look forced," Duke reminded him. "We're not even supposed to look like military.

The government made it a requirement of us going in."

Politics. Heath suppressed a sigh. The situation in the country was unstable with migrant workers, who made up the majority of the population, wanting better working rights. Things were close to the tipping point, and they'd received word a protest was planned any day now. The government didn't want to admit the workers had such organised numbers, or that it would be an issue, but had permitted Australia to land a plane at the international airport in order to get its people out.

Their one condition was that no one leaving the airport could be dressed as military personnel. The requirement was business suits, with body armour underneath, and concealed weapons—playing the role of businessmen.

"Threaten to leave them behind," Romeo suggested.

Heath studied the man. He was new to special forces and part of the second team working with them. He had a lot of time for him though. Romeo was Mila's brother, a woman they'd rescued on a previous mission, and who had earned his nickname by putting Dobby in touch with his sister after the mission. Slightly younger than the rest of them, he had an enthusiasm the team had since lost, but was sensible as well.

"Or to shoot them," Radar said with a grin.

Heath chuckled. Radar had little patience for idiots.

Dobby rolled his eyes. "Let's try Romeo's suggestion first and then Joker's."

"So when we get split up because this idiot won't leave without a fight, what do we do?" Axle asked.

They continued to brainstorm all eventualities for several hours until they were satisfied they had options for everything.

"All right," Dobby said. "Good planning. Get some rest. We'll land in five hours."

Radar swore and glanced up from the computer he had in front of him. "Dust storm is forecast."

"When?" Dobby demanded.

"Mid afternoon."

Which would make things tight. The plane wouldn't be able to take off, and dust storms could last for days in the Middle East.

"Right." Dobby's tone was grim. "What do we do if it hits early?"

They spent another hour planning before Dobby gave them leave to rest.

Heath yawned as he left the conference room. It had been the middle of the night when they'd received the call to mobilise, but at least they'd scored a Boeing jet for the trip which was used to fly dignitaries around the world.

Far more comfortable than their usual transport.

"Ready for dealing with annoying officials?" Radar asked.

"They'll be fine," Heath responded, hoping he was telling the truth. "They requested the extraction."

"There's always one pompous prick who doesn't agree," Radar said. "Just you wait." And with that warning, he settled into his seat and strapped in.

Heath shook his head.

"Think he's right?" Romeo asked from behind him.

"Yep. How are you feeling about your first special ops mission?"

"Excited. Nervous. I don't want to let you guys down. You've been working together for so long..."

Yeah, they understood how each other would react in every situation. "You'll get there," Heath assured him. "This should be a simple mission with no stealth required. In twenty-four hours you'll be disappointed with how underwhelming it was."

Romeo grinned. "Fair enough. Thanks."

"Anytime." Heath strapped into his seat, wondering whether he'd really jinxed the mission.

Chapter 2

The plane arrived right on time at the international airport. Six black sedans waited just off the tarmac, and in a matter of minutes they were driving down the surprisingly quiet roads towards the embassy.

Heath's gut clenched. "This isn't good."

"Our contact says the government is barricading the streets," Dobby reported over the ear comms. "We'll need to go the long way around. The protests are centred around Amiri Diwan." He was in the car in front. There were two special forces soldiers in each car. The convoy looked like exactly what it was: diplomatic cars driving to the embassy.

May as well paint a target on their backs.

Several other countries had already closed their embassies amid threats of sweeping blackouts, no sanitation, and violence. Without the migrant workforce, the country would come to a standstill.

Heath scanned the area, watching side

streets and the few other vehicles on the road were locals heading out of the city.

A terrible sign.

"The embassy confirmed they're ready?" Heath asked.

"Copy. We should be in and out, back at the airport by thirteen thirty."

An hour and a half on the ground. That would be a record. And the dust storm was due to hit around fourteen hundred.

The closer they got to the embassy, the more vehicles were on the streets. Most of them were beat-up vans or buses, all heading towards the parliament.

Heath swore.

"They're not interested in us," Radar said as he kept an even distance behind the car in front of them.

That might be so, but Heath didn't want to get caught in the crossfire. At least the Australian embassy was a reasonable distance from the protest, though the protest was between them and the airport.

The first car pulled into the security checkpoint, and the gates to the underground car park opened. Up ahead stood two people with archive boxes and computer equipment piled up next to them.

From the briefing, Heath knew the elevators

required a security pass to get between the floors.

As Radar pulled in behind the last car, Heath spotted people coming out of the elevator carrying boxes. Already the first cars were being loaded up.

The Ambassador and his family were bundled into the first two cars, and by the time Heath got out and joined the teams loading the vehicles with essential documents and equipment, the first three vehicles were full.

Dobby spoke with Stefan, the man in charge of the day-to-day operations of the embassy.

"Everyone here?" Dobby asked.

"Everyone except Zoe Yelton," Stefan spat out her name. "She decided it was more important to say goodbye to her friends than to help pack up the office."

Heath remembered her photo from the planning session: late twenties, short dark hair, big brown eyes, and a wide smile.

"She said she'd be right here, but I've called her twice more and she hasn't answered," Stefan continued.

"There's your douchebag," Radar murmured as he grabbed two bags and loaded them into the next car.

"Joker, you and Radar head to the lobby and look for Zoe." Dobby turned to Stefan. "Was Zoe on foot?"

He nodded. "She was on the Al Corniche about two kilometres away, so she should be here by now."

Not good. She could have been caught up in the protest.

Stefan passed him a security pass. "This will get you to the twenty-first floor in case she arrived and went straight up."

Heath took it and jogged up the stairs to the lobby with Radar behind him.

They came out next to the elevators into a curved and empty lobby. But nearby someone was gasping for breath.

Heath exchanged a look with Radar and placed his hand on his gun. He followed the curve of the wall around to the next bank of elevators as one of them dinged to announce it had arrived.

He moved faster in time to see a dark-haired woman dash into the open elevator. "Zoe!"

She glanced at him, eyes wide, and then lunged for the elevator buttons. "I'll be right back."

The doors closed and Heath stabbed the button, but he was too late. The high-speed elevator was already moving. He swore.

"You want to match for it?" Radar asked.

Heath shook his head, watching the numbers

to make sure it stopped on the twenty-first floor. "I'll go. You head back to the others and help. Let me know if I miss her in transit." He tapped his earpiece.

"Copy." Radar jogged back to the stairs as an elevator arrived at the lobby.

Heath swiped the security card and hit twenty-one on the control panel. The door closed and the numbers climbed quickly. At the eighteenth floor, the lights suddenly went out, and the elevator came to a halt. Heath stumbled at the change of speed and swore.

Someone had to be kidding him.

"Blackout," Dobby's voice came over the comms. "Looks like the entire block is out."

So he either had to wait for the backup generator to come on and hope he didn't miss Zoe, or pry open the door and jog up the stairs.

He pressed the door open button in case it had any residual power.

Nothing.

He reached into one of the inside pockets of his jacket and pulled out his multi-tool.

"First convoy has left," Dobby reported. "Joker, sitrep."

"Stuck in the elevator around the eighteenth floor. Zoe probably made it to the twenty-first before the power went out." He opened the maintenance panel underneath the buttons and triggered the manual release.

"Duke, go check the maintenance room," Dobby ordered. "Make sure the backup generator comes on."

"Situation is looking dicey on the street," Romeo reported. "More crowds gathered and a couple of military trucks."

"Cars all loaded," Axle reported.

Shit. They were waiting for him and Zoe. Heath pried the elevator doors apart, and slowly they slid open.

"Maintenance room is damaged," Duke reported. "Backup generator isn't coming back on."

There were a set of shaft doors right in front of him. He reached up and triggered the interlock. The click opened the doors partially and he pushed them the rest of the way. He was on the nineteenth floor. He leapt out and started for the stairs. "I'm out. Heading for twenty-one to get the target." But running down twenty-one flights of steps would take time, and Zoe was already puffing from her run back from her meeting. It would take them at least five minutes.

"Looks like they're preparing to close the airport," one of the team members from the first convoy said. "We got through, but there are military vehicles behind us."

Not good.

"Dust storm is coming in fast," another said. "Probably hit thirty minutes earlier than forecast."

Shit. That would make it tight for take-off.

"Heath, ETA," Dobby demanded.

There were cars in the car park he could borrow. "Go," he said. "I don't have eyes on Zoe yet. We'll meet you there."

"Copy."

It showed how worried Dobby was that he didn't argue.

"I'll leave the key decoder by the elevator," Axle said.

"Thanks." It would allow him to bypass the security of any modern vehicle. Heath burst through the doors on the twenty-first floor and headed into the embassy. He scanned the desks, but it was Zoe's frantic voice that told him where she was. "Please help me."

Who was she talking to?

He strode into the office where Zoe was on a landline and frantically stuffing her laptop and a few folders into a backpack.

"They're being transported tonight," she said in Arabic. "You must believe me. Those kids will disappear."

Heath's gut clenched. What the hell was she talking about?

"Exit street blockaded," Axle said in his ear. "Taking route B."

Right. "We need to go," he told the woman as she spun around, eyes wide, to face him. Her dark brown eyes pinned him with a plea as she spoke. "Please. Promise me you'll do it."

Heath almost nodded before he realised she was speaking to the person on the phone. He blinked, breaking the spell, and in two steps he pressed the disconnect button.

Horror filled her eyes. "You don't understand—"

Heath took her elbow, and she scrambled to grab her backpack with her other hand. "What I understand is this whole situation is moments away from combusting and we need to get our arses out of here."

He dragged her out of the room and down the corridor. "En route with Zoe," he reported.

"Find a motorbike if you can," Radar said. "Most of the streets are blocked. We're going the long way around."

"Copy," Heath said. Another option might be a boat if he could find one fast enough to cut across Doha Bay. He switched on the small but powerful torch he had stashed in his pocket as he pushed open the door to the stairwell.

Zoe was puffing behind him, saying something, but he paid her no mind until he caught the words, "people trafficking".

His pulse leapt, but he didn't slow his pace down the stairs as he glanced at her. "What did you say?"

Desperation covered her face. "Tonight. Six children. The *Tridant* container ship."

That wasn't his mission, but his thoughts flashed back to two decades earlier, their frantic flight from his country of birth, the people who promised them safe passage and then reneged on that promise.

Huddling in the dark with his younger sister while his mother paid for their safety with something she shouldn't have had to give.

"Shots fired," Axle reported.

His friend's voice cut through the memory, and he refocused on the mission at hand.

From the inside of the stairwell he couldn't hear anything, so he couldn't work out how close the fight was.

Behind him Zoe slipped on a step with a shriek, and he turned just in time to catch her, bracing her warm body against his for a second until she righted herself.

"You OK?" he asked, pausing for a second to allow her to get her breath back.

She nodded. "What's the rush?"

He started moving again. "Shots have been fired. The military are going to close the airport and streets are blockaded. It'll be hard to get to the plane."

"It's dangerous?"

"It's unpredictable." Heath didn't want to frighten her, so she didn't want to leave the building.

His calves burned by the time they reached the tenth floor, and he checked on Zoe. "You doing all right?"

She nodded, but didn't speak, waving him on.

Good. Perhaps she understood the seriousness of the situation.

When he finally pushed open the door which led to the basement car park, Zoe stumbled into him, grabbing his arms to stop from falling. Her face was pale and her breaths were pants.

He reached for his water canteen, but it wasn't there, one item which had been considered too military to be allowed as part of their cover. However his pockets were stuffed with things he normally tucked into his fatigues.

He passed her a whisky flask which he'd filled with water, and she took a sip and then bent over, gasping for breath. "Stay here. Rest."

Heath scanned the car park, but all was silent. There were several very expensive cars, but closest to the elevators was parking for the motorbikes, and there was a brand new, top of the range, bright red Ducati.

He picked up the tool Axle had left for him and assessed the bike as he crossed over to it. It didn't have a pillion seat, but Zoe was small and should be able to squish behind him. The bike had road tyres with no clamps or locking mechanisms. It would be fast.

No helmets, but not an issue. He plugged the key scanner in and set it going, scanning the rest of the car park again.

The main gate was open, possibly stuck that way when the power went out. From here he could hear the murmur of a crowd, but it wasn't close enough to be of concern yet.

The light illuminated green, and he hit the start button, grinning as the engine roared to life. He tucked the tool into his inside pocket and pushed the bike around to Zoe.

She stared at him wide-eyed as he got on.

"Come on." He waved to her.

She stepped cautiously forward, her eyes running over the bike. He answered the question in her eyes.

"There're no foot pegs. Wrap your pants and tie them." He handed her a couple of cable ties. "Get on behind me. Scootch as close as you can and keep your legs against mine." He gave her an apologetic smile. "It won't be comfortable, but we need the flexibility of the bike. If your legs get tired, tell me. Whatever you do, don't kick the back tyre."

She glanced at the tyre in question, concern on her face, before nodding and swinging her leg over the back, pressing her body against his. Her soft breasts warmed his back. She wrapped her arms tightly around his waist. "Ready."

"Hold on," he called, and slowly accelerated to get a feel for what the engine could do.

It was feisty, and he grinned, keeping the speed as slow as he could and called to Dobby, "On the move."

He turned away from Doha Bay, moving north before he turned west to meet one of the main roads which ran through the city.

"Stay clear of the US embassy. Protesters are surrounding it as well," Dobby called.

He visualised the map he'd studied during the planning. It was on the route he'd planned to take, but he could turn off early. "Has the embassy got help?"

"Yeah, I spotted Rambo's team as we drove past."

Good. They'd worked with the SEAL team before on joint exercises, and the guys were excellent. As much as he wanted to help them, it wasn't his mission or jurisdiction to do so.

The streets were clear, and he turned the throttle, giving the bike its head. Zoe's arms tightened around him, but she didn't say a word.

He glanced down streets as they drove past, and saw a crowd in the distance, but he kept going. At this speed, they might catch the convoy. They were about ten or fifteen minutes ahead.

He counted the passing streets and made note of the signs, slowing to turn left towards the Doha Expressway. They sped away from the US embassy and back to the D Ring road to the airport.

"Situation at the airport is worsening," Romeo called.

Heath slowed so he could hear better.

"They're closing the runway," Duke replied. "Dust storm is visible on the horizon."

Fuck. Could anything else go wrong?

"Five minutes out," Dobby reported.

"Fifteen," Heath added. So much for the easy mission for a change. He shouldn't have jinxed it. Behind him Zoe shifted, but it was enough on this bike at this speed to make him battle for control. When he regained it, he reassessed their options. No point killing themselves to make it on time.

Romeo's voice came over. "They've given us clearance to take off if we go now. Wind's picking up."

"How much time before it hits?" Dobby

demanded.

"Ten, maybe fifteen minutes," Romeo said.

They wouldn't make it, and the conditions would prevent the plane from taking off if they waited. The situation on the ground could escalate further, particularly if the storm lasted for several days.

"Go," he said. "Take off as soon as the rest of the team arrives."

"Heading through the entrance now," Dobby reported. "What's your plan?"

"Plan Charlie." They could be in Saudi Arabia in a little over an hour and a half after the dust storm had blown over. Or, if the storm settled in for several days, they could get a car or boat and exit the country.

"We'll organise you both visas for all surrounding countries," Dobby said.

They both knew Heath could get into the country without going through a checkpoint, but it would be good to have the option of going right up to the border crossing, and would help with them getting out of that country.

Visas were a future problem.

Right now, they needed to find cover before the storm hit. He slowed his speed.

"What's happening?" Zoe yelled over the engine noise.

"Change of plan. We need to find shelter."

They were surrounded by light-coloured, high-density housing without a garden or shelter to be seen.

"There's a souq not far from here."

A public space, but people might be hiding at home. It gave them a much better chance of changing vehicles and getting supplies. If he could get them a decent car, the dust storm wouldn't be a problem. "Which way?"

She shouted directions at him, and he drove fast through the streets. The scent of dust floated on the increasing wind as he turned into the car park. Zoe was off the bike almost before they stopped.

They dashed inside as the first wall of sand hit.

Heath winced. The shiny, brand new bike wouldn't look so shiny or new by the time the storm finished. Hopefully the owner had good insurance.

"We're in the air," Dobby said.

Good. At least his team was safe.

Inside the souq was a warren of shops full to bursting with clothes, spices, souvenirs, and anything he could need.

He grinned. Time to kit up.

***

Zoe's legs screamed at her as she limped away

from the door of the souq. Wind and sand rattled the glass. Thank goodness they were no longer out there. She turned to the man who had dragged her out of the building and onto a motorbike, studying him for the first time.

The dark business suit made him look like a bodyguard and a foreigner, but his dark hair, thick beard and tan skin said his heritage was probably from around this area.

He scanned the area, looking for threats.

She tilted her head. "Do we have time for some introductions now?"

He glanced at her, confused for a split second, and then grinned. "I know you're Zoe Yelton, political analyst, and the person I thought would be the least pain in the arse on this mission."

She frowned, but the teasing way he said it made it impossible to be angry by the assessment. "And you are?"

"Joker."

She raised an eyebrow. "Joker? Is that all I get?"

He moved through the aisles between the stalls and stopped at one that sold camping supplies. "It's my job to get you out of here safely since we missed the extraction."

She gaped at him. "They didn't wait?"

"Couldn't with the dust storm incoming. It

would have put everyone at risk."

Taking care of the majority. But she'd put Joker at risk. This was what happened when she disobeyed her superiors. Would she ever learn? "I'm sorry."

He nodded an acknowledgement as he placed a backpack, rope, and a bunch of random looking things in a pile and spoke flawless Arabic to the shop owner, asking for a price.

She could be flying over the country right now, rather than wearing sweaty clothing in the middle of a souq in a country which might erupt into violence at any second.

But if she was here, maybe she could help the children being trafficked. She studied Joker as he bartered the price. He was more than a bodyguard; of that she was certain. She'd overheard one of her colleagues mention they were sending in special forces just in case. And he'd started the motorbike with some kind of fancy gadget.

Joker handed over cash and stuffed his purchases into his backpack before slinging it onto his back. "This way."

He led her to a stall selling loose-flowing traditional clothing. He held up a top against himself and then pants and added them to the pile before he turned to her. "Do you know how to wear a hijab?"

She nodded. "But what I'm wearing is appropriate attire."

"It is." He added a hijab and a black abaya to the pile. "But we need to blend in more."

He purchased the clothing and gestured her towards a curtain at the back which was some kind of change room. As she watched, he emptied his jacket pockets of various items and then stripped it off. Underneath he wore a bulletproof vest. He glanced at her. "Hurry up."

Definitely prepared for the worst. Just how dangerous was it out there?

Her mind whirled as she took the clothing behind the curtain. They had no rendezvous, the dust storm would make it far easier to sneak into the port, and the protests would mean fewer people at the docks. It was the perfect opportunity.

But that would be going against instructions again. Dare she risk it? She slid the abaya over her existing clothes and swapped her scarf for the hijab. Both items were heavier, but also somewhat comforting. Quickly she stuffed her scarf into her backpack and swung it onto her back. She stepped out of the change room to find the shop empty except for the owner.

Her pulse jumped. Had Joker left her here?

"Where did my friend go?" she asked the man

in Arabic.

"He said he would be right back."

So she was just supposed to wait here for him and hope he was telling the truth?

Why wouldn't he? She was his mission, even if she was a pain in the arse.

She tapped her thigh as she stood at the front of the stall, waiting. There weren't many people around; some gathering supplies like Joker had, others waiting by the entrance looking out at the dust storm, and a few stall owners locking up for the day.

One minute became two, and then three.

Zoe's chest tightened. Where was he?

How long should she wait before she made her own plans? Nisha lived nearby, so she could always try her place, but the dust storm would make it difficult to navigate.

Just as her pulse rate was increasing, she spotted a man striding towards her. She almost didn't recognise Joker. He hadn't gone for the traditional long thobe, but wore long pants and shirt, and could have passed for both a local or a migrant, definitely blending in.

Zoe let out a sigh of relief. "Where have you been?"

"Getting supplies," he said, gesturing to his far bulkier backpack. He glanced at her clothes and nodded. "Looks good."

She warmed at his compliment and followed him out of the shop. "Joker," she began and then stopped. "I'm sorry, I can't call you that. What's your real name?"

He glanced at her. "If I told you that, I'd have to kill you."

She rolled her eyes and waited.

He grinned, seemingly pleased by her reaction, and the smile made her heart rate increase. "Heath."

The name suited him. "Heath, what's the plan?"

He led them through the souq as if he had a destination in mind. There were so few people inside and some stalls were closed, but the coffee stall where Heath finally stopped had a couple of stools outside. "Coffee?"

She nodded, frowning. What had happened with getting out of town quickly? She sat and waited until he brought the thick, dark coffee to the table along with a couple of syrupy dumplings.

"What intel do you have about the children?" Heath asked.

Zoe blinked, surprise filling her. She'd thought he hadn't been interested and she'd have to convince him. "Photographs," she said. "And a firsthand witness confirmation of what occurred."

He gestured to her backpack. "In there?"

She fumbled with the zip and dragged out her laptop. "Nisha was going to send the photos to me. I met her down on the Al Corniche this morning. It's why I was late."

While she waited for her laptop to boot, he said, "Tell me exactly what she told you."

"Three boys and three girls were picked up in fancy cars by people promising to get them well-paying jobs in Saudi Arabia, but Nisha's son followed the car and it went straight to the port where they were loaded into a container."

"How did he get access to the port?"

"He works there." She found the email and opened it, turning the laptop so he could see the images.

Heath's frown deepened as he zoomed in on the photo of Maryam looking worried. "When's the ship due to set sail?"

"Nisha said today, but it's probably delayed due to the protests and the dust storm."

He nodded and took out his phone, searching for something. "Where does Nisha live?"

"In Asian City, not far from here." Hope stirred. "Can we help?" Zoe sipped the coffee, bracing for the jolt of caffeine while she waited for his answer.

"It's not my mission," Heath replied, but he sounded more like he was trying to convince himself of that.

"Isn't it everyone's mission to stop children from being treated as slaves?" she challenged, trying to hold back her ire. She needed him on her side.

"Yeah," he said. "We're going to need a car."

Chapter 3

Hope filled Zoe as she beamed at Heath. "We're going to rescue the children?"

He pressed his lips together, and Zoe was momentarily distracted. They were very nice lips; plump and luscious. Heath had looked suave in his business suit, but now there was an edge of danger to him.

"They may have been moved," Heath told her.

She blinked, taking a second to remember what they were talking about. "We can find them. I gave them my mobile. It has a GPS tracker on it."

Heath took out his phone. "What app?"

She told him the name. "Everyone at the embassy has to use it in case we run into trouble." Kidnapping was a risk that had been raised when she'd accepted the job.

Heath downloaded the app and took a bite of his dumpling. "It won't be long before the government shuts down all communications, but GPS should still work." He handed her the phone. "Log in."

Quickly she did so. She clicked on the marker. "Here. They're still at the docks."

"Assuming your phone reached them." Heath took the phone back, glanced at the screen and then swiped away, pressing some buttons.

Her gut clenched. He was right. While she knew and trusted Nisha, there was no guarantee her son had given Zoe's phone to the children.

"Is your friend taking part in the protest?" Heath asked.

"I'm not sure."

"Do you have her number?"

Zoe nodded. "It's on my… phone." Which she no longer had. She really had to look into backing it up to the cloud. Something on her to-do list which never seemed particularly urgent until now. "We could visit her."

Heath grunted, neither agreeing with nor dismissing the suggestion. "We don't have a lot of time. The dust storm is either going to smother the protest or allow the protesters to overrun areas." He shook his head as if he couldn't believe he was doing this. "We don't know whether they've taken control of the port, or if the ship will sail during the storm… we know almost nothing."

"Nisha might know more."

He sighed. "What about Nisha's husband or friends? Are they likely to see us as bargaining chips?"

Surprise filled her, and she considered the question carefully. "I don't think they will, not if they know we're trying to help the children. One of them is Nisha's niece."

Heath finished his coffee. "We need to move."

She gulped the rest of her drink, wincing at the taste, and grabbed a dumpling from the plate. "Where to?"

He handed her a pair of goggles before looping another pair around his head and pulling up a scarf he'd wrapped around his neck. "We'll find a car first, then we'll go to your friend's place. If she's not there, we move on to the next plan."

"Which is?"

"I'll tell you when I make it up." His eyes crinkled to show he was smiling underneath the scarf. "Pull the goggles up and cover your nose and mouth. It might be hard to breathe outside. Stay right behind me."

She nodded. She'd witnessed dust storms from the comfort of her office or apartment before but had never gone out in one.

Zoe packed her laptop and swung the bag over her back. As they stepped outside the building, the wind hit her, along with tiny pricks of sand hitting her hands and clothes like a swarm of unhappy bees. Thank goodness she had everything but her hands covered, because the sand stung.

Heath headed straight towards a white sedan that had to be over twenty years old.

The sand blotted out the sun, turning the day dark with an orange tinge, and no one was within the thirty metre diameter of her vision.

Heath jimmied the lock and then reached over and opened the passenger side. "Get in."

She hurried around the other side and leapt inside, relieved to be out of the wind and dust. She inhaled deeply, which set off a series of hacking coughs.

"Keep your breaths shallow for a minute," Heath said as he fiddled with a tool. In a matter of seconds, the car started.

"What is that?" Zoe asked.

"Fancy tech," Heath said, slipping it into his pocket. "This car isn't as sophisticated as more modern ones so I could have hot-wired it, but this causes less damage." He glanced at her, his goggles and scarf still in place. "Which way?"

Zoe took a second to get her bearings and then pointed. "Down there, and it's the second or third street to the right. I'll know it when I see it."

"If you can see it," Heath pointed out.

He was right. The haze and dust made it almost impossible to see anything. She held her breath as he pulled onto the main road but there was no squeal of brakes or loud crashes. He accelerated, but only fast enough not to be a hazard and she stared out at the street, trying to spot the building she used to tell her when it was time to turn. Normally she was coming from the city, so they were almost past it when she recognised it. "Here."

Heath turned the wheel, executing a near-perfect hand brake turn as he headed down Nisha's street.

"It's just up ahead." She leaned forward to get a better look. "On the left." She pointed, and Heath parked in front of the door on the opposite side of the street.

He placed a hand on her arm. "You need to follow my lead in there," he said. "If I say go, we go. If I tell her we have a full team of soldiers waiting for us, you nod in agreement. If I say bark like a dog, you bark, got it?"

She cracked a smile, but heard the seriousness in his voice. "Woof, woof."

"Good. Let's go."

***

Heath hoped he was doing the right thing. He should have got the supplies, stolen a car, and got the hell out of the city, but the whole time he was in the souq he couldn't stop thinking about the children.

The stalls reminded him of a peaceful time as a child when he'd followed his mother through the labyrinth of shops to get the day's groceries. Though even that was marred as he searched the faces of men, looking for one with a hooked nose and missing finger, who'd changed his world forever. It was a habit he couldn't drop whenever he was in the Middle East.

He remembered the terror of their flight out of the country and the helplessness of being unable to control their fate. He couldn't let another child go through that. Not when he had the skills to do something about it. So instead of accompanying Zoe safely out of the country, he was heading into a building with an unknown number of potential hostiles.

Not his best day at obeying orders.

What he could see of the street was empty. Anyone who supported the uprising was either at the protest or sensible enough to get out of the storm. Perhaps if Zoe was safe at Nisha's place, he could go alone, rescue the kids, find transport for him and Zoe, and then come back for her. A good option, but his mission was to get the embassy personnel home, and leaving Zoe unprotected, even if she thought she was safe, did not sit well with him. There was no telling what Nisha's husband would do, and whether he would want to use them as leverage.

But the other option was taking Zoe with him, and while she had done what he'd asked of her thus far, she didn't have the skills to help with the rescue.

At least the dust storm gave them cover. Zoe knocked on a door of a downstairs apartment.

A female voice called in Arabic, "Who is it?"

"Zoe."

The door swung wide and a short Pakistani woman stood there in a bright blue sari. "Have you got the children?" Her eyes widened as they fell on Heath, but she ushered them inside, looking over their shoulders for more people.

Heath stepped inside and moved down the corridor to give her space to close the door against the wind.

The noise outside muted as he took in the area. The apartment was small with two rooms on each side of the corridor, the first on the right a sitting room which contained an older man with his foot in a cast, perhaps Nisha's husband, and three children ranging in age from about ten to fifteen. He continued down the corridor, taking in a kitchen area and two bedrooms, all empty.

Returning to the sitting room, he nodded at the man and pulled down his scarf, lowering his goggles as Zoe made the introductions.

"Why are you here?" the husband, Adnan asked.

Zoe glanced at Heath.

Good. She remembered what he'd said. "Would you prefer we speak in Arabic or Urdu?" Heath asked.

The man raised his eyebrows. "Urdu."

It was a test, almost a challenge, but Heath had no problem conversing in either language. And this way he could fill Zoe in on only what she needed to know.

"My mission is to get Miss Yelton out of the country," he said. "But she told me about the children who are being smuggled, one of whom I believe is related to your wife."

The man nodded.

"I would like to help them if I can, but I need information."

"Why would you help?" Suspicion creased Adnan's face.

"Because your people helped my family when we fled Iran." Without their help, his family might not have survived.

The suspicion faded somewhat. "What do you

need to know?"

"Do you know the protesters' plans?"

"They were marching today, and I can't march with them." He gestured at his broken foot.

"Just in the city, or at the port as well?"

"They left the port to protest in the city. It should be empty aside from those in charge."

Good. "Any security?"

"They may have locked the gates and have people guarding it."

He needed up-to-date information. "Is your son still at work?"

A nod.

"Can you contact him?"

Another nod, and Adnan drew out a phone from his pocket. A few moments later, he was explaining the situation to his son. He then handed the phone to Heath.

"Salam Alaikum," Heath said. "Did you give Zoe's phone to the children?"

"It's on their container. The container has been loaded onto the ship."

Damn it. "When? How? I thought the workers had left the port."

"There are a few who did not attend the protest, and the ship was already at dock."

"When is it due to sail?"

"As soon as the paperwork is done."

Heath made a note of the time. It would be at

least a thirty-minute drive to the port from here. "Will they set sail in the dust storm?"

"I heard someone say the storm doesn't extend far over the ocean. They can use instruments to make sure they don't hit anything."

"Are there many more containers to load?"

"No. They're done. The cranes can't operate in a storm."

That wasn't great. "Can you delay them?"

"No, sir. I don't have any authority."

"Can you get us close to the ship? Is anyone guarding the entrance to the port?" Could they even get there in time?

No answer.

"Hello?" He glanced at his phone. The call had ended. He called back but got an error message. Networks were down. The government had shut down communications. He swore and handed the phone back to Adnan.

"Heath?" The quiet question in Zoe's voice made him turn to her. She waited, her hands clutched together.

"Communications are down," he said in Arabic so they all understood. "The ship with the children on board is due to set sail soon."

"Can we do anything?"

"Maybe." He wouldn't promise anything. "But

we need to get to the port."

A burst of gunfire outside made Heath dive for Zoe, covering her body with his and pushing her away from the window.

Her shriek was cut short as he shoved her against the wall, his gaze going to the window. From here all he could see was the dust cloud.

Zoe gave a slight groan, and he realised he was pushing hard into her soft body. He shifted away and looked down at her. "You OK?"

She nodded, her eyes wide. Was that a flicker of awareness in them?

Before he could fully process it, one of the children whimpered.

He spun to find Nisha and her family on the floor, looking at him for direction.

Perhaps it was just a protester letting off his frustration. He held up a hand for them to stay where they were and shifted to the window to peer outside.

At the edges of visibility rushed a body of people, and he could hear the cries of alarm over the wind.

Really not good.

Who were they fleeing from?

He didn't think they would have reached the suburbs so quickly, unless they were the protesters who'd been outside the US embassy.

They could have made it in time.

There was no way the American soldiers would have opened fire on the protesters. That would have started an international incident, so it had to be someone else scaring the workers away.

"Do you have a back door?" he asked Nisha.

She nodded. "But it leads to a small courtyard. The only way out of the complex is through the front."

"What about over the wall?"

"It's into the opposite apartment's courtyard."

Of course.

He continued monitoring the situation outside as an army truck rolled past with armed Qatari soldiers in defensive positions.

They must have protected the US embassy, but they wouldn't have done so for nothing. Perhaps the US government had promised help in exchange for their people's safety.

It didn't matter. What mattered now was getting out without being shot and reaching the port in time.

"Do you have a vehicle?" He couldn't risk getting to the one parked outside. Chances were high that the street was blockaded.

"No."

Damn. Without his team, he had no extra eyes, intel or backup.

If the ship wasn't leaving, he would stay here until the situation blew over. But the children were in danger.

There was no way the Australian government would greenlight a mission to rescue a few non-citizen children from a cargo ship, or even from the destination port. If he didn't get to them now, they were lost.

Would Zoe be safer here or with him?

Who knew what the military might do? Some governments had been brutal during the Arab Uprisings in 2011, but Qatar had not.

If he left Zoe here, it might be difficult to come back for her, and he wouldn't be able to protect her.

And that was his mission. If they couldn't get into the port, he'd head for the border with her and they would be safe.

"We need to go," he told her. "It won't be pleasant. We have to go on foot until we find another vehicle."

"Can't we use the one outside?"

"Street will be barricaded and they might open fire on anyone trying to leave."

"What about those leaving on foot?"

He pressed his lips together. "I'm hoping we'll be fine."

"Hope?" Her expression was justifiably incredulous.

"There are no guarantees, but we need to take calculated risks." And he hoped the dust storm would hide them and that the military had only left a small guard at the street entrance. He turned to Nisha and Adnan. "If we get the children, can your son bring them home?"

"He catches the work bus, but they should be able to take them," Nisha said.

All right. That meant they could head for the border from the port. The plan crystalised in his mind, and while he didn't have the time to plan for every option like he would for a normal mission, he had enough fallbacks that he was comfortable. "We won't be able to contact you after we leave," he said. "But we'll do everything we can to get those children."

Nisha clasped his hand. "Thank you. May God shine over you."

Adnan nodded his agreement.

Heath turned to Zoe. "Goggles on, scarf up, and same goes. I move, you move."

She nodded though she was a little more wary.

He flashed her a smile. "Don't worry. I can do this with my eyes closed."

Her smile was a little forced, but at least it was there.

Chapter 4

Zoe's heart rate increased as she stepped out into the dust storm behind Heath. The reality of the situation she'd got them into was sinking in. The wind battered her hijab and clothes, but thank goodness Heath had bought them goggles to protect their eyes.

She took shallow breaths through her mouth, adjusting the bottom of the hijab like a filter against the thick, suffocating dust.

Heath was already several steps in front of her and almost out of sight. She hurried to catch up with him as they walked down the wall of the apartment block, her eyes straining to see movement around her. The street was empty as far as she could see, and no more military vehicles drove past. But would any soldiers shoot people on sight?

Her shoulder muscles tightened as she waited for a gunshot.

Heath held up a hand, and she almost ran into him, too busy scanning her surroundings to watch him.

He steadied her with one hand, his eyes on something at the edge of visibility ahead. Zoe squinted and could barely make out the shapes of something in the dust.

Heath pulled out his gun.

Zoe jolted. She didn't know he even carried one, but he must think there was a threat to have it out. He took her hand with his free one and bent to murmur close to her ear, "Move with me."

She nodded, taking comfort from his strong, warm grip.

He turned his attention back to the shape, and she braced herself. When he tugged her hand, she was ready, and she followed him step for step, first moving slowly and then a few fast steps that brought them to the edge of the building and around the corner.

Zoe tensed, waiting for a shout or a shot, or some other indication they had been spotted, but there was nothing. It wasn't until Heath slowed that she allowed herself a breath of dusty air, her hijab filling her mouth as the wind blew it in. She adjusted it.

Heath squeezed her hand and she loosened her grip. Poor man would have bruises.

Heath kept them moving, but said, "How many blocks to the edge of the suburb?"

"About four."

He nodded in response and she guessed he was planning something. The military could have blockaded the Asian City and industrial area which was where most of the migrant workers lived. If they had, there'd be no point getting a car, but they were also running out of time to get to the kids before the ship sailed.

Another shadow materialised out of the gloom, this time a car. Heath stopped and jimmied it open. "Get in." He checked the time. "Quickly."

She ran around the other side of the white hatchback and got in. Heath had already got the engine started.

"Move the seat back and get on the floor. Brace yourself and stay low."

Her hand shook as she adjusted the seat and squeezed herself into the footwell. She ducked her head and braced a hand against the seat and the centre console.

"Good. Don't move until I tell you."

The sounds of the call to prayer were just audible above the wind and the sudden sound made Zoe flinch. She closed her eyes, her heart racing as Heath drove. He wasn't going fast, maybe because of the lack of visibility, but then he swore, and the car shot forward. Zoe braced harder as shots rang out and the windscreen exploded.

She gasped, but Heath didn't flinch or slow. The car bumped over something, maybe a curb and her body banged against the dash. She gritted her teeth at the pain and glanced up at Heath. Wind blew his scarf against his mouth and his gaze was focused on the road, but his shirt had torn along his bicep, and a red patch seeped through the black.

He'd been shot.

The car jolted again, and she hit her head against the door, wincing and repositioning her hands.

"Stay down," Heath yelled.

"You've been shot." She didn't have a first aid kit. What if he bled out? She didn't know where the nearest hospital was.

"Just a scratch," he replied as he pushed the old car as fast as it would go. "We're clear. Sit on the seat and strap in."

Zoe's hands trembled as she shifted to the seat and fastened her seat belt. The windscreen had several holes with webbed cracks stretching out from them.

They were on a long flat road with dust surrounding them. Best she could tell they were out of the city and crossing the long, empty stretch of desert between the city and the new port.

"Are you OK?" Heath asked.

She glanced at him. "That should be my question. You're bleeding."

He checked his arm where the patch of blood had stopped spreading and patted it with a wince. "Just a graze. It looks worse than it is, but it stings like a mother-fucker."

She felt his grimace rather than saw it.

"We don't know what reception we're going to get at the port," he said. "There might be guards, or the government might not care."

"So what's the plan?"

"The windscreen with bullet holes in it isn't a good look if there are military guards, but if they're migrants, they should let us in."

"So what, we have to wait until we arrive before you make a decision?"

He nodded. "Stay strapped in for now. If there's military on the gate, our story is, you're my wife, and I've brought you here where I think you'll be safe. Keep your head lowered and your scarf high so they can't see your face."

"What about you? If there are workers on the docks, they'll think you're the enemy."

"Then I tell them the truth, that we're here to rescue the children."

It seemed reasonable, but there were so many variables. Perhaps he was hoping she didn't realise that, so she didn't worry. He certainly sounded as if he had everything under control.

Calm, unbothered.

It worked. Her heart rate slowed a little. Whatever happened, Heath would be able to handle it.

The dash clock showed it had only been about twenty minutes since they had left Nisha's place. The speedometer was straining at a hundred and twenty kilometres an hour.

She prayed they didn't meet another car on the road because there was no way Heath would stop in time.

Her eyes strained to see through the dust cloud for any light or shadow which could indicate someone else was out there.

Nothing.

They might as well be the only people on earth.

She kept scanning until the first structure appeared and Heath slowed. The main entrance had a security boom gate and several military personnel stood outside, in the storm, rifles at the ready.

Zoe's heart pounded. Were they about to be shot?

Was this the last thing she would ever do in her life?

At least she would die knowing she was trying

to help.

Heath's chuckle pierced through her fear and she glanced at him as he pulled to a stop outside the gate and wound down his window a crack.

What was so funny?

She glanced at him and then remembered she wasn't supposed to let them see her face. She lowered her head.

"Who did you piss off to get the shit job, Fox?" Heath asked.

Zoe jolted. He knew the soldier? She lifted her head so she could see.

"Who the hell are you?" The soldier's American accent made her relax slightly.

"You wound me," Heath replied. "It's Joker, Squadron 6."

The man's tone shifted. "They leave you behind?"

"Got split up. Need access to the port to rescue some kids who are being smuggled out of the country."

"You need a hand?"

"Wouldn't say no, if you've got spare men."

Fox said something into his radio and two men came out of the guard house and got into the back of the car. Heath greeted them as Fox raised the boom gate and waved them through.

Heath wound up the window and drove

forward. "Long time no see," he said to the huge men in the back. "Zoe, that's Rambo and Phoenix."

"Nice to meet you, ma'am," Rambo said. "What's the mission?"

"Find the *Tridant*, get the kids out of a container and back home to their parents. Then get Zoe here out of the country. What are you doing on guard duty?"

"Military helped at the embassy and got our people to safety in return for us staying here and helping," Phoenix replied. "You're the first people we've seen out here."

Rambo drew out a radio and spoke in Arabic, asking for the location of the ship. Within minutes they had the dock coordinates.

"Can we talk with the ship's captain?" Zoe asked. "Maybe if he sees you, he'll let the children go."

"Or maybe he doesn't know what cargo he's carrying," Phoenix said.

"Then surely he'll let us search," Zoe said.

Heath shook his head. "We've got no jurisdiction and he could get into trouble opening a container without due cause."

She stared at him. "Don't you think trafficking children is due cause?"

"Joker's right," Rambo said. "We go in with demands and they're likely to say no just to spite us."

"So what do we do?"

"Ship's registered in Iran." Phoenix gave Heath a look.

He stopped the car on the edge of the container area and glanced at her. "Can you protect Zoe while I'm gone?"

Zoe shook her head as a glimmer of fear filled her. "No. You're not leaving me behind. Those kids might not want to go with you. I've met Nisha's niece. She'll know it's safe if she sees me."

"He'll work much faster without you there," Rambo said.

Dread lodged in her stomach. She didn't want to be separated from Heath. He'd got her this far. She didn't know these men, though they seemed nice and were probably capable if Heath was going to leave her with them.

But then it was her fault they were still here. "Maybe it hasn't been loaded on to the ship yet."

"They've finished loading," Heath told her.

Rambo's radio blared with voices. "Hostiles incoming. Need backup."

"Out, Zoe," Heath barked and she jumped, shoving open the door as Heath leapt out of the car and Phoenix jumped in the driver's seat. Rambo shoved her out of the way and in seconds they were speeding back to the entrance.

Zoe exhaled and moved over to Heath, glancing back towards the car which had already disappeared in the dust. She placed a hand on her heart to help calm it. "Holy crap you guys are fast."

Heath chuckled. "We've got to be." He also glanced back to the entrance. "Looks like you're staying with me."

Relief filled her though she didn't like the grimness of his tone. "Do you think they'll get in?"

"I don't know. Let's move." He grabbed her hand and kept her by his side as they crossed over to the massive cargo ship that was docked beside the equally massive yellow cranes that were motionless in the storm.

There was no way they would find the right container. The ship was massive, and containers were stacked ten high and who knew how many wide, not to mention those below deck.

"We won't find them, will we?" Zoe asked Heath, her heart sinking.

"Your phone is still giving off a strong signal, and I made note of the container number in the photo you had. That gives us the coordinates."

She had no idea. "But it might be below the deck, or out of reach?"

"Yeah." He glanced at her but it was impossible to read his expression. "Here's the thing. The chances of us getting on the ship, finding the kids, getting them out of the container and off the ship before the ship sails are slim."

Zoe wanted to be sick. "So we have to leave them here."

He hesitated. "There's another option."

"What is it?"

"Each ship has enough lifeboats for its crew," Heath said.

She frowned as she tried to follow his train of thought. "So what, we steal one of those after we get the kids?"

He nodded.

"Do you even know how to launch one?"

He placed a hand on his chest. "Darling, you wound me."

His attempt at humour made her smile. "Sorry, I forgot you're special forces. Does that mean you can do everything?"

"Pretty much."

His confidence made her smile and settled her stomach. "All right. What do we do?"

Chapter 5

Heath studied the woman crouched down beside him in a dingy area of the ship. She hadn't hesitated throughout this entire mission. He'd thought she'd baulk at the thought of being stranded at sea, but she'd agreed with very little hesitation.

They'd sneaked onto the ship after he'd found some high-visibility shirts and hard hats and the crew were all busy lashing down containers and finalising paperwork to question why two other people were boarding.

Now they were near the reefers, or refrigerated freezer containers, which wasn't the best place to be because crew would be around to check them regularly. The container they were looking for was towards the bow so they would have to move, but not until they were underway. He couldn't risk them being caught and thrown off the ship.

The ship's frame blocked most of the dust storm, leaving them with the smell of salt and diesel, but at least there were fewer particles in the air. He lowered his scarf and took a couple of deep breaths.

"What now?" Zoe asked as she adjusted her hijab.

He hadn't had a chance to pull up the ship's schematics, identify any hidey holes or any of the usual things he did prior to a mission, but the ship was like one he'd worked on before. One of the lockers just below deck was their best bet until they were underway, because there were only long gangways down the port and starboard sides and nowhere to hide from the crew who would be doing last-minute checks.

It would be a squeeze, but there was no reason for the crew to check them now. "This way." He took her hand to keep her next to him and pulled her along, down some stairs and along a tight corridor until he spotted a sign that said Pollution Locker.

Perfect.

He opened the door and squeezed inside. The walls were lined with absorption material, boxes and hoses, ready for an emergency if the ship had an environmental spill like oil or fuel. The absorption material had the bonus of muffling some of the sound of the engine, which was firing up. He pulled Zoe in after him and closed the door.

"Why are we here? Can't we try to get the kids off before we leave the dock?" She glanced around the small space, urgency in her voice.

He shook his head and kept his voice low. He doubted anyone would hear them talking over the hum of the engine, but it paid to be careful. "Too many people are on deck doing final checks. If we get caught, they'll kick us off. We don't know if the crew is aware of the kids, and they won't open a container just on our say. It's not worth their jobs."

Concern covered her face. "Then what do we do?"

"Make ourselves comfortable," he said, shifting past her so he was between the door and her. He gestured to a crate in the corner for her to sit on. "When we get underway, the crew will break into their shifts. Some will head to their cabins to sleep before their shift starts, and others will begin their rounds. We wait for an hour, when things should have settled, and then we go."

Zoe lowered herself onto the crate, her face creased in a frown. "So we're stealing a lifeboat?" She clutched her hands together and exhaled as if bracing herself.

He nodded. "We'll get the kids into the boat, lower it into the water and head to shore."

"Back to Qatar?"

He pressed his lips together. "Maybe. I'm hoping to get in touch with my team when we get into international waters." He smiled to remove her worry. "I'll figure it out."

She nodded slowly as if not quite convinced.

Now wasn't the time for her to underestimate him. He needed her to react fast, do exactly what he said, when he said it, without question.

He needed her trust.

"Look, I get that it sounds unconventional, but I'm trained for this. There are always things you can't plan for, but I'm great at responding to changes." He smiled, hoping to put her at ease.

Zoe exhaled. "I understand, but this is my first rodeo so to speak."

He nodded. "And you're doing great so far." Heath grabbed a bucket and moved it closer to the door so he could sit. Time for some get to know you, so she didn't question everything he did. "Tell me about yourself. Where are you from?"

"Born and raised in Perth."

"That's where I live now." He smiled. "Which suburb?"

"Fremantle."

He glanced at her. Short dark hair, hazel eyes. "Italian descent?"

"Yeah. The weekend treat was going to

Gino's." She gazed towards the door, a smile on her face, not really in this room. A picture of serenity now he'd distracted her from what came next.

"Best coffee in the city." Gino's was an institution that had been there for decades.

"Damn straight, and I'll fight anyone who denies it." Her smile hit him like a burst of sunlight.

He shifted back at the force of it, his heart racing in response. He cleared his throat. "Siblings?"

"Three sisters. You?"

"Younger sister."

"What does she think about what you do?" Zoe asked.

He grinned, thinking about Leila. "I'd like to say she thinks I'm a bad ass, but in truth, she most likely thinks I'm crazy."

Crazy for risking his life mission after mission after he'd almost lost it as a child. Though she understood his need to protect others from experiencing the same terror they'd gone through.

"I'm sure she's very proud of you."

"She's over in London doing a Masters in Political Science and Law. She's so smart." And trying to fix the injustices in the world through talk and diplomacy.

"Is she considering getting into politics, or does she want to join foreign affairs?"

"Depends on the day I speak to her and what's happening in the world. She's got more causes and ideas than she has minutes in the day." His heart swelled with pride.

"I can put her in touch with some people if she wants to go the embassy route," Zoe said, then grimaced. "Assuming I still have a job when this is over."

More kindness. "That's a nice offer. Thank you." It also brought about a nice segue into what he wanted to know. "What made you ignore orders and your own safety to rescue a bunch of kids you don't know?"

She shrugged and fiddled with a loose thread from her hijab. "It was the right thing to do."

He shook his head. It wasn't that simple.

"Are you suggesting I shouldn't have tried to save them?" Her voice rose with incredulity.

"No, it's not that. You should have alerted authorities, but not everyone would have taken the time to meet Nisha, particularly when they'd been ordered to pack up." He tilted his head. "Why did you?"

"Because she's my friend, and she was desperate. You don't just leave your friends like that." She hesitated, before firmly pressing her lips together.

He was curious about what she was going to add, but he left it. Her beliefs in supporting friends was something Heath believed down to his core, but over the years he'd discovered not everyone had the same values. His respect for Zoe grew.

"I agree. That's why I know, as soon as they can, my team will look for us." He met Zoe's gaze and saw she understood.

"Thanks, Heath. For believing me and for helping me. I know this isn't what you expected on this mission."

He shrugged. "I always expect the unexpected, but I'm damned glad those protesters were more organised than we anticipated, because I wasn't sure how I was going to save the kids from Australia."

Another sunbeam smile and he felt like a hero. "You wouldn't have forgotten about them?"

"Never." The engine tone changed and there was a slight shift. "We're moving." Which meant the crew would start heading below deck soon.

He checked the time. Still a few hours before dark, but the longer they waited, the further from the coast they would be. They could make their way to the United Arab Emirates, but it would take longer to get the children back to their parents. Qatar would probably be closer anyway and they could then make their way to the Saudi Arabian border.

"Should we go now?" Zoe asked.

"Let's wait another half an hour," he said. "So they can settle into their routines." He was tempted to leave Zoe here where she should be safe, but the thought of not having eyes on her at all times made him uneasy.

And if she was caught, they'd question her and radio the mainland to send out a boat to pick her up. Then he'd be in a real rush for time.

He visualised the ship. It was about a hundred and fifty metres to the container they were after and their only option of hiding would be ducking behind pillars.

"How are we going to get the container open?" Zoe asked.

"I know how to work the lashing rods," he replied. One unlashed container shouldn't affect the stability of the others, particularly as it was in the middle. One of the crew would find it on their next rounds and fix it.

"Then we take them to the lifeboat?"

He nodded. Trying to sneak half a dozen kids to the lifeboat would be the difficult part. If the crew spotted someone, the alarm would be raised and he doubted they'd let him steal a lifeboat.

This had to be a non-lethal mission. None of

the crew might know what they were carrying. They were just doing their jobs.

But if they were caught, he needed to make sure they could both escape. Which meant he needed to prepare Zoe in case they got separated. He glanced over her clothing. Her outfit was bulky enough that she should be able to hide a few things, and he'd bought extra at the markets in case things got worse.

He handed her a small multi-tool. "Take this."

"Why?" She examined the tool, pulling out the knife.

"You might need it. Just in case."

"You think I might need to protect myself?"

"The hope is you won't need to. It's a backup. If we get locked up somewhere, you'll have a tool which might help you get out."

"This assumes I don't get locked up with you," she pointed out as she tucked it into her pocket.

"Always planning for contingencies." He pulled out some cable ties and a small ball of rope. Glancing up he was met with Zoe's round bottom bent towards him as she picked up something from the ground.

Despite the layer of fabric, heat shot through him, but it took him a second before he could tear his eyes away from her. She placed the item on the shelf and turned back to him. He swallowed and handed her the cable ties and rope.

She raised her eyebrows. "Do you want me to tie you up?"

The image seared his brain, and he fought back a smile. "Not today. But if you need to restrain someone."

She stared at him. "What do you expect me to do? Say 'wait a second while I retrieve my knife to threaten you and then hold still while I tie you up'?"

He did laugh this time. "You never know what situation might arise, but no, that wasn't my thought." He hesitated before unzipping a small side pocket in his backpack and drawing out a sealed packet of white powder. He'd been surprised to see it being sold, but it was another contingency.

Zoe frowned at him. "What's that?"

"It's a sleeping powder." He'd recognised the name from his time in Iran. "A mouthful of this will knock someone unconscious." He hesitated, not wanting to tell her she might want to use it herself if the situation got really dire. He cleared his throat. No, he wouldn't let it come to that. "You might get an opportunity to put it in someone's drink. Then when they fall asleep, you can tie them up."

She looked dubious, but took the packet, untied her abaya, and tucked the packet into her bra. "What's the likelihood of that?"

"Slim, but you never know."

She studied him as she slipped the rope into her pocket and then slid the cable ties into her bra as well. "How much darkness have you seen?"

The quiet question struck him like a dart on a bullseye. "Too much," he replied. "But I've seen extraordinary good done as well, like what you're doing for these kids."

"I couldn't do it without you." She reached out and squeezed his hand, and her touch branded him. "Thank you."

He gently pulled away, suspecting he was falling under her spell. "It's the right thing to do."

He checked the time. They could go. He stood. "Follow me." He pulled up his mask again, and Zoe quickly retied her abaya and adjusted her hijab.

He cracked open the door of the locker and peered out.

Empty.

He gestured for Zoe to follow and stepped into the metal corridor, hurrying to the door that led to the starboard deck.

Over the loud whirr of the engines, he heard voices coming from the intersection ahead.

He grabbed Zoe's hand and pulled her through the nearest doorway. It was a tight squeeze, being some kind of cleaning locker with barely enough space for two people. He pulled her against his chest and rotated them so he was next to the closed door. He turned, facing the door, keeping one hand behind him, touching Zoe's waist so he knew where she was, and the other reached for his gun before he stopped himself.

Non-lethal mission.

The voices passed by and he relaxed and turned, and realised his hand was positioned possessively on Zoe's waist. Heat seared him and he snatched his hand away. "Sorry."

"It's fine." Her voice was breathy.

Great. He'd just assaulted the person he was trying to protect. "Really. I needed to know exactly where you were."

"I know." Was she disappointed?

His body stirred as he turned away. "Let's go."

He peered out the door and, seeing no one, stepped out.

When they got to the outside gangway, dust still filled the air. Thankfully they still had their goggles and scarves. Heath checked the phone GPS as he passed row after row of containers.

They passed a storage box full of lashing rods, and he grabbed the spanner-like tool that tightened them together.

He found the row that corresponded with the

number he'd noted and peered along it.

Empty.

Good. He headed down, checking the column numbers as he did.

The GPS corroborated the location. Somehow Nisha's son had got them the phone.

He strode along the corridor, scanning for grey containers and checking the numbers on the sides to ensure he'd got the coordinates correct. Sure enough, the container was right in the middle on the level they were standing on. Perhaps so that someone could check on the kids during transit.

It made this a hell of a lot easier.

He checked in both directions and then knocked on the container door. He wasn't expecting a response and wasn't surprised when he didn't get one.

"Is this it?" Zoe whispered, her excitement palpable.

"There may be no way to get to them," he warned. "Any number of boxes could be packed in front, or they may be locked in a compartment at the back." He surveyed the position of the lashings and the door latches and noticed a lumpy bit of duct tape tucked in one of the grooves at the bottom. The colour blended nicely with the metal and looked like rubbish unless you were looking for something specific.

Heath grabbed the loose bit of the tape and peeled it off.

Zoe's phone.

He handed the phone to her.

"He didn't give it to them." Worry filled her voice.

"He probably didn't get the opportunity, but it was quick thinking to tape it to the outside of the container. We know we've got the right one."

"But they don't know we're coming for them."

He smiled. "Then we'll be a nice surprise." Heath glanced up and down the corridor. Without knowing the routine on the ship, he didn't know how frequently the crew would do their checks.

Quickly he undid the lashing rods in front of the container door before opening the container. The door opened enough to squeeze in if he took off his backpack.

He shone the torch through the opening and illuminated plastic-wrapped pallets stacked in place, two high and two wide with a gap at the top which might be wide enough for him to squeeze through. They were also tied in place on the interior of the container to stop movement during transit.

He whirled around at the sound of voices.

Two crewmen were working their way up the corridor, checking the lashings. It would be easier to evade them without Zoe.

"Get in." He held the container door as wide as it would go and cupped his hands to boost her inside on top of the pallets.

She took off her backpack, throwing it on top, and then let him help her inside. "I'll be back for you." Before she could protest, he shut the door and locked it.

Time to hide.

Chapter 6

The click and slide of the bolt being put into place was full of menace. Instant blackness surrounded Zoe as she lay on top of the pallets, heart pounding. What the hell just happened?

It had been too fast for Zoe to process. All she'd known was that when Heath said something, she had to act.

So she had.

But now she was in the pitch black, surrounded by metal and squeezed in the tiny gap between the pallets and the roof.

She hadn't had a chance to mention her real fear of small, dark spaces to Heath.

Her heart beat even faster and her breath quickened, sweat breaking out over her skin. She was alone, stuck in this hot metal container, and there was no way she could get out by herself. What if Heath didn't come back for her? What if the container tipped over? What if the boat sank?

Her chest tightened and her fingers clenched.

A scream tickled her throat just wanting to be released. She couldn't stay here. She had to get out. Zoe scrabbled backwards and her feet hit the door, the clang resonating throughout the container.

"Help!" The cry was faint, but Zoe clung to it as she wrestled the panic back.

She wasn't in a mine shaft. She hadn't defied her parents. Heath knew where she was. He would come back to let her out. She squeezed her eyes closed and imagined being in a meadow full of flowers. She inhaled deeply and then exhaled, counting to ten. There was still a hint of dust in the air, but not as thick as it had been that day in Coober Pedy.

She shoved aside the memory with another inhalation and slow exhalation as she tried to get her brain to override her body. It wasn't her poor decision that had got her here, it was Heath boosting her in.

Though they wouldn't have been here if she hadn't been late to the rendezvous. So it was another poor decision, thinking she knew better. Would she ever learn?

"Is someone there?" The faint words were in Arabic, but they were enough for Zoe to be sure someone was in here.

Her decision would protect several children, and that cry for help had to be from one of them.

Zoe cracked open one eye and was met with darkness. She had to go with what she had seen in the split second the door had been opened and Heath had helped her inside.

Two pallets high, two pallets wide, and who knew how many pallets deep. Her head brushed the metal ceiling. Would she get stuck if she shuffled further?

She gritted her teeth and inhaled again, slowly exhaling and willing her body to relax.

Heath would come back for her.

She was not stuck in here. She would not suffocate. She would not be crushed.

Each thought helped to calm her, and though her skin felt tight and her heart still raced, she reached out a hand and brushed her backpack. She shifted it to the side and pulled herself forward.

Heath will come for me.

She stretched her other hand out and grabbed some of the plastic covering the pallet and gripped it.

Heath will come for me.

She pulled herself forward, sliding across, the plastic screeching in protest.

Heath will come for me.

She stretched out her other hand and pulled herself along the top of the pallets. Repeating the mantra over and over, she slowly slid her way across until her hand met open air. She wasn't at the end of the container, but there was definitely not another pallet below her. She needed light.

Her phone. Heath had passed it to her before he locked her in.

She slid her hand awkwardly down the side of her body, hampered by the lack of room, and fumbled for her pocket, finally finding the opening. Her fingers brushed the warm phone and she gripped it, bringing it around to the front and turning on the torch. Light filled the space, making her blink at its brightness. When her vision adjusted, she discovered a gap only a metre wide before the wall of the container.

An empty gap.

Her stomach dropped.

They weren't here.

So where were they? She was sure she'd heard a voice.

But had that been a product of her panic?

Had she brought Heath on this mission for nothing?

She closed her eyes as the enormity of the situation smothered her.

They were no longer rescuers, they were stowaways who would have to steal a lifeboat in order to get off the ship and home.

A lifeboat which might save someone's life if

the ship sank.

How was she supposed to face Heath now?

A slight movement, enough that her body felt it, reminded her she was on a ship getting further and further out to sea. And she was locked in a container with very little space.

As the claustrophobia threatened to take over again, something banged against the side of the container.

She flinched as another clang sounded.

What the hell?

Understanding hit her.

The crew had found the lashings undone and were retying them. She was really stuck in here.

She flicked off the torch and squeezed her eyes closed. She was fine. Heath would come. He would let her out. And she'd definitely heard a voice. That was not a hallucination of her panic. Which meant she had to find the kids before Heath returned.

Exhaling a shaky breath, she shone the torch around the space.

A smear of something dark—paint, or maybe blood—was in the far corner. It was probably left there from when the container was built.

"Hello?" she called. There'd be another twenty-foot container behind this one, so she didn't have to worry about being heard. She reached across the gap and tapped on the wall.

It sounded kind of hollow, not like solid metal. To compare, she tapped the side of the container and it was more of a clunk.

"Help us," a young child called in Arabic. The call was faint, but it was coming from the other side of the back panel.

Elation filled her. She'd found them. "I will," she promised. "How did you get in there?" She searched the wall looking for a latch or a gap she could get her fingers behind to pry open the panel.

"They forced us in."

Zoe shuffled to the other corner and couldn't see anything that indicated a door or any kind of entry. "How many of you are there?" she asked as she continued to search.

"Twelve."

She paused. That was far more than she'd expected. They must be crammed in there like sardines. Would they all fit in the lifeboat?

"But the others are not awake."

Zoe bit her lip as she tried not to think the worst. "Can you wake them?"

"No." His voice held tears.

"Did the people who took you give them anything?"

"They gave us dates to eat, but I'm allergic, so I didn't eat any."

"Did the others go to sleep after eating them?"

"Yeah."

OK, so maybe they were just drugged and not dead. But that would make it a hell of a lot more difficult to get them to the lifeboat.

One problem at a time.

First she had to get them out.

There weren't any gaps between the walls she could get her fingers into.

She glanced at the door. Where was Heath? Surely he had evaded the sailors by now.

She turned her attention back to the wall. There had to be a hinge somewhere. "Where is the door?"

"They moved a whole wall."

Oh shit.

Zoe examined it. Could she peel it open from the top or sides? She highly doubted Heath would have something that would cut metal in his arsenal of tools. The bottom of the wall was flush with the floor, but a shadow appeared at the top when she shone her light on it.

"Are you still there?"

"Yes," Zoe called. "I'm trying to work out how to let you out." She reached out for the small, shadowy area. Her fingers curled around the edge of the wall.

Yes.

She tugged down, the metal biting into her fingers, but it barely shifted.

"I can see some light!" the boy cried, his voice full of hope.

Would she be able to get him out? She tugged again on the metal and it shifted a little, but there was no way she was going to be able to peel it back like opening a tin of tuna. She slid her fingers along the top to the corner and felt around for some kind of latch. "What's your name?"

"Mohammad."

"Nice to meet you. My name's Zoe. I've got a friend who will come to help soon and we'll get you out." Somehow.

Her fingers found a metal lump, and she ran her fingers over it. Was it a lever? Stretching her fingers, she felt and heard the release. Tugging hard, the wall shifted towards her and then hit the pallet.

"You did it!" Mohammad yelled.

Except there wasn't a gap to squeeze past. All she'd done was give the children more room. And most of them were unconscious.

She glanced back towards the doors, but they were still closed tight. How long before Heath was back?

"Mohammad, could you try to wake the others again? Maybe shake them gently and call to them."

More people to put pressure on the door

would be useful.

Mohammad called, and Zoe heard rustling, which indicated he was shaking them. Someone moaned.

"Wake up, wake up," Mohammad shouted.

Another groan.

"Mohammad, is there any water in there?" She held the torch up to the gap to illuminate the space.

"No. There's just a bucket."

Perhaps the container was getting off at the first stop. At least they'd provided a toilet. "OK."

She checked the battery on her phone. Fifty percent. The torch was running it down fast.

"Is it just one person waking up?"

"Two," Mohammad replied. "The rest won't wake."

She hoped they weren't dead. The smugglers would want them alive, but what if they'd miscalculated the drug dose.?

"Do you know any of the other children?"

"Iman's my cousin. She's waking. That's all I know."

"Great. Keep trying. I'm going to pry the door open." What she needed was a crowbar or some kind of lever. Something like the lashing bar spanner. Heath must have taken it with him. She yanked on the corner of the door again, but it didn't move.

There was nothing she could do.

They were stuck.

***

Heath kept close to the containers, moving in the opposite direction to the sailors who were checking the lashings. The men were focused on the job, but Heath was still forced to go slowly so as to not attract attention. He lowered himself to the main deck and the dusty sea air hit him in the face.

Carefully he made his way along the side of the ship, back towards the lifeboat he'd spotted earlier. With the container identified, he wanted to plan their escape in more detail before he returned.

The closest lifeboat was almost a hundred metres from the row of containers the kids were in. Depending on their condition, some kids might need to be carried, but he hoped most would be able to walk.

The fewer trips they had to make, the better.

He couldn't prepare the lifeboat for deployment yet, in case one of the sailors noticed and started monitoring the area more closely.

The GPS on his phone told him they were heading towards Iran and it would be touch and go which country they'd be closest to by the time they got the kids out of the container.

He ducked behind a beam as he heard voices approaching and checked his watch. The two sailors walked past talking about dinner.

Hopefully that meant they would pause their patrols until everyone had eaten, but they might eat in shifts.

Heath remained crouched and monitored the aisle he came out of until the sailors who had been checking the lashings emerged and then turned down the next corridor heading towards the bow.

He checked the area for anything that might be useful. It was empty. This ship obviously had high standards for keeping the deck clear.

At least he still had the lashing rod spanner and the lashing rod. Heath headed further away, keeping his eyes peeled for any sailors who might be doing rounds, and identifying nooks they could hide in if necessary.

There weren't many hiding places despite the size of the ship because most of the deck was taken up by containers. He passed another lifeboat, checking it as he went by so he had an alternative if there were issues with the first one.

He doubted anybody on board the ship would care to go after them. They probably didn't even know what cargo they carried.

So that just left him to decide which country

to go to once they were free. Perhaps phone service would work the further away they got from Qatar, and he'd be able to call his teammates and they could organise a rendezvous for him somewhere.

Voices sent him back into the shadows underneath a set of stairs. Another pair of sailors talking about dinner.

Time to return.

He didn't spot any sailors on the way. The men who were checking containers had at least another fifty metres to check before they'd head back in his direction.

Not a lot of time.

He climbed the short ladder to the row he needed and jogged along it until he came to the container.

Which had the lashing rods back in place.

Damn it.

Quickly he unbuckled them again and pried open the doors, using the buckles to hold the doors open. Enough light flooded the container for him to see Zoe still on top at the far end, but no one else.

Zoe glanced at him, eyes wide. "Heath."

Her relief and the fear in her eyes hit him in the gut. "I'm here. Did you find the kids?"

"Yeah, but I can't get the door open. I need that spanner."

Heath glanced in both directions. Empty. He didn't want to get into the container and risk them both being locked inside. "Come back here and keep watch." He took his backpack off and leaned it against the side of the pallet.

"Heath will help you, Mohammad," Zoe called and shuffled backwards on the pallets towards Heath.

He helped her down. "What's the situation?"

"There's a metal wall between us and the kids. Mohammad is the only one conscious. I think they drugged the rest of them, but a couple are stirring. I found a latch, but it doesn't open far enough to get them out. We need to pry the metal down."

Crap. They would have to carry the kids to the lifeboat. "How many?"

"Twelve."

Double crap. Depending on their sizes, he might be able to carry two at a time, but it would require both of them to get the kids on top of the pallets and pull them out. He glanced in both directions again. "Keep watch. If anyone comes this way, tell me. We should have a bit of time."

She nodded and took a couple of deep breaths as she took position next to the door.

Heath threw the spanner on top of the pallets and hauled himself up.

Damn, it was a tight fit. He sucked in his

stomach and pulled himself over the pallets, shoving the spanner forward with him. Finally he reached the end and shone the torch along the metal wall. He spotted where it had moved and was resting next to the pallets.

He shuffled closer and shoved the tensioner through the small gap. It was just wide enough.

He yanked down and winced at the screech, but at least it opened.

"You're doing it, Zoe!" The excitement in the boy's voice killed Heath.

"Hey, Mohammad. I'm Heath," he said in Arabic. "We'll get you out shortly. Can you tell me about you and the other kids? How tall are you?"

"A metre twenty," he said proudly.

"How many others are as tall as you?" He shoved the tensioner further along the wall and pulled down again.

"The boys are all smaller," Mohammad said. "The girls are taller."

"How many boys?" Again he moved the tensioner along and pulled down. The gap was widening.

"Six, and six girls."

There'd be plenty of room in the lifeboat, but it would take time to get them there. The longer it took, the more chance they would be spotted.

A girl groaned and Mohammad said, "Wake

up, Iman. We have to go."

Heath continued along the top of the door, prying it open all the way. "Is anyone else conscious?"

"A couple of the girls were mumbling, but they didn't make any sense."

But they might be able to move when the time came. "Zoe, throw me a bottle of water from the bag." He shoved the next section down and turned back as the water bottle landed next to him.

He shone the torch over the gap. "Mohammad, I'm going to drop a bottle of water. Can you reach up and catch it?"

Small hands reached up, and Heath dropped the bottle into them. "Give Iman a sip. Not too much. We don't want her to choke. Then give the other girls who are awake a sip as well."

"Yes, sir."

Heath dragged the final bit of metal down so there was a gap of about forty centimetres. Not a lot, but it should be enough for the kids to fit through. "Can any of the girls stand?"

"I can," a female voice said.

Heath shuffled forward so his chest was over the empty space and peered into the secret room. A girl no more than about thirteen shifted to her feet, with Mohammad supporting her. "Well done. Now reach your arms up. I'm going to pull you over."

The girl swayed, her eyes not really focusing.

"Reach up," Heath encouraged.

Mohammad helped her lift one arm, and she lifted the other herself. Heath stretched out and clasped her wrists. This position sucked, but there was no other choice.

He pulled, using every muscle in his chest and arms to drag her over the bent metal edge. When her belly rested on it, he shifted further back and dragged her the remaining distance, so she lay on the pallet in front of him.

"You did it!" Mohammad cheered.

He had, but it would take a hell of a lot of muscle power to do that eleven more times. The girl blinked at him.

"What's your name?" he asked.

"Iman."

"Great, Iman. I'm Heath. Zoe is waiting outside. Can you crawl forward for me?"

She nodded, though her gaze was still a little glassy, and inch by inch she crawled forward.

This was going to take too long.

He shifted to the back of the container. "Mohammad, I'm going to drop you down the torch. Can you see if anyone else is waking up?"

"Another two girls are staring at me."

"Great. Give them some water too."

What he needed was someone on that side who could help lift the kids to him. Mohammad wasn't big enough.

Behind him, Imam hadn't reached the end of the container yet, moving as slowly as a sloth. Damn it.

"New plan, Mohammad. I need you to come out next."

"What about the others?"

"We'll get them, but I need you to be my eyes outside. Keep watch for anyone coming."

"Bad people?" The fear in his voice made Heath want to hit the people responsible.

"No, just the crew. We're on one of those big container ships."

"Why?"

"The bad people put you here, but we'll get off as soon as we get everyone out."

"How?"

"Lifeboat. It'll be cool, but I need you to leave the water and torch inside and jump up and grab my hands." Heath held out his hands, and after the second attempt, Mohammad grabbed them.

Heath hauled him back, and Mohammad kicked to help. The kid weighed only about thirty kilos. "Great work. Now crawl to the end. I need you to watch over Imam and keep watching both directions. If someone comes, you call me straight away, all right?"

Mohammad nodded and scrambled across the pallet like a lizard, reaching the end just after Imam lowered herself to the ground.

"Zoe, I need you in here," Heath called.

She hesitated. "Why?"

He would have missed the fear in her voice if he hadn't been expecting her to agree immediately. He twisted so he could see her better. She stared into the container as if it was the last place she wanted to go.

But she'd already been in there.

"I need your help to lift the kids from the other side." He kept his tone gentle, removing the frustration. "Think you can do that for me?"

She nodded, bracing herself as if facing a firing squad. "You won't close the doors again?" She climbed up on the pallets.

Oh hell. "Don't you like the dark?"

She shook her head. "I'm claustrophobic."

And he'd left her there by herself. "I'm so sorry. I wouldn't have left you if I'd known."

She gave him a half-smile. "There wasn't a lot of time to talk." She dragged herself next to him and looked over at the other space.

If there was more room in the container, he'd get into the secret compartment, but Zoe wouldn't have the upper body strength to pull those kids out. "Can you be brave for me again?”

She nodded. “What do you need me to do?”

“Lift the kids as high as you can so I can grab them. If they’re conscious, they might be able to help. You might be able to give them a leg up.”

“We’re going to have to carry them to the lifeboat,” Zoe said.

“Yeah, but we’ll deal with that next. Some of them might be awake enough to walk.” Or hold themselves up in a piggyback.

Zoe nodded and lowered herself into the compartment.

Chapter 7

Zoe fought the urge to cringe as her feet touched the floor in the hidden room. She was even deeper in the container, and it would be more difficult to get out. The walls radiated heat still, and the smell of sweat was strong. Breathing through the anxiety, she glanced around. The torchlight illuminated ten children lying on the ground, some of them on top of each other, with barely any room to stand.

Her fear vanished, replaced by heartache. She needed to get these children out of here.

A young girl, about twelve years old, blinked at her.

Zoe crouched down and smiled. "Hi. I'm Zoe. I'm going to get you out of here. Can you stand for me?"

The girl frowned but didn't move.

Heath said something in another language, and the girl looked up and then shifted.

"What did you say?" Zoe asked as she pulled the girl to her feet.

"The same thing you did, but in Urdu."

Of course. Some of these kids might not have had time to learn Arabic. The girl moved slowly as if not in control of her body and leaned against Zoe. Luckily she hardly weighed anything.

Heath called something, and the girl lifted her hands above her head. "I'm going to ask her to jump. Put your hands on her waist and help hoist her when she does."

Zoe did as he asked, noting another girl was moving, prodding Maryam next to her.

At another command from Heath, the girl jumped. Zoe lifted her, and when Heath clasped the girl's hands, she let go and used her back as a bench so the girl's knees would rest on them and Zoe could help lift.

Once the girl was out of the compartment and while Heath spoke to her, Zoe turned and helped the next girl to her feet. "Just a sip." She passed the water bottle to Maryam and checked the boys. None of them had stirred, but they were much smaller than the girls. The drugs might take longer to wear off.

"Mohammad, there's some food in my backpack. Share it with the girls, but just small bites," Heath called.

Together they lifted the remaining four girls out of the space. Maryam frowned at her in vague recollection, but Zoe didn't push it. She'd introduce herself when the girl was more alert.

The boys hadn't stirred, and Zoe bent to check their pulses. Slow, but there.

She glanced up at Heath. "How do you want to do this?"

"Can you lift them?"

She studied the boys, choosing the smallest one, and bent her knees and lifted him under the knees and back. She stumbled into the wall and steadied herself. "Now what?"

"How good's your deadlift?"

She laughed. "Non-existent." But there had to be some way to get the boys out of here. She jiggled him. "Come on, wake up." She tapped his thigh, trying to get a reaction.

The boy groaned.

"That's it. Wake up." She jiggled him again, and his eyes opened. Confusion crossed his face. "Hey. My name is Zoe. I'm trying to help you, but I need you to reach your arms up above your head."

A frown.

"Mohammad, do you know the names of the boys?" Heath called.

"Faizan," a girl called back.

The boy looked up towards the voice. "Imam?"

"She's on the other side of this wall," Zoe told

him. "I need your help to get you to her. Hold your hands up high."

Faizan did as she asked and she jiggled him about until she could get him into a position where she could jump and Heath could grab him.

By the time his feet cleared the edge of the wall, Zoe was panting. She couldn't do that for four more boys. She crouched down and moved them all so they weren't lying on top of each other. Then she tapped and sprinkled water on their faces, hoping to get some kind of reaction.

Heath slid into the compartment behind her. "Swap places with me. I can lift them so they're over the wall. Then you just need to pull them over into the gap. When they're all out, we can lift them onto the pallet."

She stood; the tight spacing meant she was pressed against him. She took a moment to draw comfort from him. They were in this together.

He ran a hand down her arm in support and then cupped his hands. "Quickly. I don't want to be in here if someone comes."

Of course. Fear gripped her, and she let him boost her up. By the time she'd turned around on top of the pallet, Heath had the next boy in his arms. He practically threw the boy over the wall, his upper body strength incredible.

The boy was alert enough to reach out his arms, and she caught him, pulling him towards the pallets.

He half-slammed into a pallet with a cry.

"Sorry!" Zoe said.

The boy scrambled for purchase and he climbed up the rest of the way, his gaze clearer.

"The others are at the end." Zoe pointed. "Wait with them."

He moved without speaking, and Zoe turned her attention back to the remaining boys. It didn't take too long to get them all out, though the last two were barely conscious and had to be dragged across the pallet to the entrance.

Heath positioned them into a recovery pose and left them lying on top of the pallet. "In case someone comes and we need to hide again."

Not everyone would fit in the small gap between the pallets and the doors, but hopefully it wouldn't come to that.

Zoe stepped out of the container and took deep breaths, relief filling her. The light was duskier now, and there was less dust in the air.

Heath did a quick headcount, assessing each child.

They all sat or slouched at the edge of the container, unable to sit upright, though Imam and one of the other girls seemed more alert.

"We're not all going to make it in one trip," Heath said in English. "Too many of them will need to be supported or carried."

Zoe nodded. "What's the plan?"

"I'll take Mohammad, these two girls, and carry a boy. I'll get the lifeboat open, and hopefully by the time I return, the rest of the girls will be alert enough to walk. I'll take them and another boy, and on the final trip, I'll carry two and you can carry one."

"I stay here with them?" It made sense.

"Yeah. I'm not leaving without you, Zoe."

She smiled. "I know. Go." The longer they stayed, the greater the chance they'd be caught.

Heath turned and explained the situation to the children.

"I'm not leaving without Faizan," Imam said, her expression fierce.

Faizan was the only other boy who might walk by himself if he had a bit more time to recover.

Heath picked up one boy who hadn't stirred yet in a fireman's lift. "Faizan can walk on the next trip."

Iman shook her head. "I can carry him." She pulled Faizan to his feet and turned around, saying something to him that Zoe couldn't hear. Faizan hopped on her back in a piggyback.

Heath smiled. "All right. Let's go."

Zoe watched them go for a second and then turned her attention to the remaining children. She handed around the water for those who could drink.

"What happened to us?" one girl asked, her speech still a little slurred.

"You were told you were going to Riyadh to work, but the men who promised that lied," Zoe told her gently. "Someone saw you being put into the container and I was contacted."

"Who are you?"

"A friend of Nisha Khan."

Maryam stirred. "My aunt?" She blinked. "Zoe?"

Zoe smiled. "Yes. She asked me to help you." She checked the row to make sure no one was coming.

"I'm Zoe," she told the others. Four girls and three boys still to move. One was conscious but not responding to anything. She moved over to him. "Hi. Will you drink some water for me?" She held a bottle up to his lips.

He pushed it away.

Maybe he was worried about being drugged again. "Do any of you know him?" she asked the girls.

They shook their heads.

"I'm trying to help you. We're getting you off this ship and back home. I need you to hold on so I can carry you."

He stared back at her uncomprehendingly.

Damn it.

She continued her rounds, making sure the last boy who was still unconscious was breathing.

One girl started crying. "I want to go home."

Zoe knelt next to her. "It won't be long. We'll get you there."

She checked each way and froze when she spotted two crew walking past at the end of the row.

She held her breath as they spoke to each other and continued walking, not looking down the row. When they disappeared without spotting her, Zoe exhaled.

They were on the side of the ship that Heath had gone to. What if they caught him with the kids?

Had there been enough time to make it to the lifeboat yet? Would the crew notice something amiss?

Her chest tightened, and she checked the other direction. Should she move everyone in the opposite direction or inside the container?

As her hands twitched and clenched, she took a deep breath. Calm down. Heath was an expert at evasion. He could deal with two crew members.

There was nothing to worry about.

***

Heath reached the lifeboat and unclipped the safety chains blocking the entrance. With the door open, he stepped back to let Mohammad and the others in first, before he handed the unconscious boy through to Imam.

He got in after them, closing the hatch and assessing the situation. There were windows all the way around, but the centre steering column would block them from sight. He took the boy back from Imam and placed him in the middle seat where he wouldn't be seen and strapped him in. Then he turned to the others. "Keep low. Don't move around, don't talk unless you have to. Stay hidden. I'll be back with the others as soon as I can."

The kids nodded.

Heath went back to the entrance, peering out the window to ensure no one was coming, and then lifted himself out.

He redid the chains so nothing looked out of place and then jogged back towards the container. Halfway there he spotted a crew member climbing down from a row.

Shit. He ducked behind a thick pillar and confirmed the sailor was coming this way before crouching low, monitoring him.

He got closer and closer, and ten metres before he reached Heath, he climbed the ladder into a container corridor.

Heath exhaled and waited a couple of beats before checking his surroundings and jogging up the gangway. At the row where the crew member was, he checked carefully, but the man was walking away from him.

Good.

Heath continued, climbing up the ladder he needed. Because he knew what to look for, he noticed the container doors were open, but it wasn't too obvious.

Zoe peered out, checking one direction and then spotting him. She stepped out and started gesturing to the others.

Heath smiled. Good. She was getting them to move.

He assessed the girls first. Two were still unsteady on their feet, leaning against the ones who were stronger, but at least they could move.

One boy was on his feet, but looked like a zombie, another was more alert, and as he reached the container, he spotted the last boy still unconscious on the pallets.

"You got to the lifeboat OK?" Zoe asked.

"Yeah. There's a crew member between us and it, but I'm hoping he'll head down the other side." Heath pulled the boy out of the container and gently placed him on the ground.

He wanted to do this in one trip if possible. He could carry two boys. "Zoe, can you carry the more alert boy?"

She nodded. "I can piggyback him."

"Do that." He placed the unconscious boy over his shoulders in a fireman's lift. "Get the girls moving. Stop at the end of the row. I'll be right behind you." He shut the container, loosely tying the lashing rods in place, and then picked up the zombie boy in his arms.

The others were halfway down the row, not moving very fast.

Hopefully with a bit of encouragement, they'd pick up the pace.

It was awkward going, and he'd have to put both boys down if they ran into trouble, but he wanted to be off this ship.

He caught up with the group and took the lead. "Faster now." He broke into a jog so he could check the gangway was empty and they wouldn't be caught.

Way too many people to protect. He just hoped the crew wasn't involved in the smuggling and therefore wouldn't try to stop them.

Heath peered down the gangway. At the far end he spotted crew members carrying what looked like a big roll of barbed wire down the stern of the boat.

Shit. They were preparing the boat for pirate waters. Maybe they weren't stopping in Iran.

Which meant they might have armed guards already on board.

Heath needed to get everyone off this boat before they went through the Strait of Hormuz and into open water.

The others reached him and Heath said to Zoe, "I'll go first. I'll tell you when to follow. You come last."

She nodded and put the boy down so she could rest.

"I need you to pass the boys down to me." He was skilled, but descending a vertical ladder without hands was beyond even him. He passed the child to Zoe, checked the corridor and then descended and held his hands out for the child again. The boy on his back shifted, and Heath jerked him back into position before taking hold of the second boy.

He moved to the closest pillar and gestured for the first girl to follow him.

One by one they descended onto the gangway, the boy Zoe had been carrying making it down the ladder on his own and then standing, staring down the passageway. Zoe followed him and shifted him out of view before lifting him in a piggyback again.

Slowly they made their way towards the lifeboat with Heath checking each row before giving them the sign to move. The crew were most likely busy at the stern, because he didn't see anyone else, but it wouldn't be long until they started protecting the sides of the ship.

He really hoped they did the port side first.

When they reached the lifeboat, Heath lowered the boy he carried to the ground. Quickly he undid the chains and opened the hatch of the lifeboat. "Inside."

The girls lowered themselves in and greeted the others.

"Sit and strap in," Heath called in two languages.

Zoe helped the boy in and glanced at the children with Heath.

"I'll pass them to you."

She jumped in and turned to him. He handed her one and Mohammad appeared to help her carry the boy to a seat.

Heath checked the surroundings. At the far end a sailor was heading towards them, but his gaze was on the clipboard he carried.

Shit. "Zoe, quick!" He shoved the other boy at her and she stumbled back, but Heath was already releasing the safety cables needed to lower the lifeboat.

He glanced at the crew. Their eyes met.

The man shouted and reached for his radio on his belt.

Fuck. Heath released the final cables and leapt into the lifeboat, shutting the door behind him. "Everyone strap in."

Zoe was still strapping in the unconscious boy. He waited a beat for her to finish and sit, then he pressed the release for the lifeboat to lower.

The cables creaked but moved fast, and he mentally thanked the crew who made sure the equipment was well maintained. The boat lurched from side to side and Heath could only see the side of the ship and the ocean through the window.

The boat jerked to a stop and a couple of girls shrieked.

Damn. Maybe there was an override on deck.

Heath scanned the controls and spotted the one he wanted. He hit it and the boat released, dropping the remaining distance to the water with a crash.

Some children screamed.

"It's all right," Heath called as he started the engine and steered the boat away from the ship. He drove straight towards the setting sun to make them more difficult to spot and checked his GPS.

They were in the middle of the Persian Gulf, pretty much at the intersection of Qatari, Iranian and United Arab Emirates territorial waters, but their options for landing included the United Arab Emirates, Saudi Arabia, Oman, Iran and Qatar.

There weren't any Australian naval vessels in the area. They'd reviewed that as part of their mission brief yesterday.

Iran was out of the question since he was a wanted man in the country due to a recent mission.

Qatar made sense for the kids, but not so much for him and Zoe.

There was an Australian embassy in Abu Dhabi, but he wasn't sure of the political implications of bringing the kids there.

He checked the ship was still on its way and hadn't done anything daft like sending another lifeboat after them.

All was clear.

"What now?" Zoe asked.

"Plan B," he said.

"Which is?"

"I'm working on it." He smiled to reassure her. Qatar was the best option for the children. He could get Zoe and himself out of there when the children were safe. He pointed the boat in that direction and tried calling Dobby. They would still be in the air but might have phone signal.

"Status," Dobby barked.

Heath grinned. "In a lifeboat with Zoe and a dozen kids in the Persian Gulf."

Dobby swore. "Why do you have a dozen kids?"

"They were being trafficked out of Qatar. It's why Zoe was late."

"Copy. What's the plan?"

No more explanation needed. That was one reason he loved his team. "Heading back to Qatar to get the kids home. Comms are out so when we get them there, we'll head for the Saudi border." He glanced out the windows and spotted a naval boat heading towards them at speed. He swore. "Zoe, get the binoculars out of my bag. What flag is on that boat?"

"Trouble?" Dobby asked.

"To be determined." He accelerated as Zoe unstrapped and dug through his bag to find binoculars. She focused on the boat. "Iranian."

His muscles tensed as he pushed the boat faster towards Qatar. "Iranian navy."

"Can you outrun them?"

"Going to try. What're the coordinates for Qatari waters?" It might not matter to the navy as there were always disputes over where the territory lay.

Dobby yelled a demand at the rest of the

team, and Radar responded with the details. Heath checked his coordinates. "We're a mile out."

Zoe glanced at him, concern on her face. He smiled. "Strap back in."

The water was choppy and the border patrol boat had a far superior engine. They were already closing the distance. They must have seen the lifeboat launch from the container ship and most probably had contacted them and discovered what had happened.

But if Heath was caught by the Iranians, this entire mission could go south immediately. He pushed the engine as fast as it could go, and Zoe stumbled on her way back to her seat.

"Status," Dobby said.

"They're quicker than us." He glanced behind again.

"Can't they help?" Zoe asked.

He shook his head and then paused. The Iranians would help Zoe and the kids. He was the only issue. "Might need to hide," he told Dobby. "Let's go with the Darius ID." He couldn't risk them finding out his true identity in case they linked it with his identity, which had an arrest warrant attached

"Copy. Give Zoe this number. One of you call us within two hours. I'll contact Arash and let him know to be on the lookout."

Their Iranian contact. Good idea. "Copy." He hung up. The boat was only a hundred metres away. They would start hailing the lifeboat soon. "Zoe, take the wheel."

"What's going on?" Mohammad asked, coming to stand with them.

Zoe took the wheel. "Keep heading there." He pointed to the compass. "That will take you back to Qatar." He wrote Dobby's number on her palm. "Memorise this. It's Dobby's number. You call him within two hours if you can. Give him an update."

While she memorised the number, he turned to Mohammad. Contingencies. There always needed to be contingencies. "I've been in trouble with the Iranian authorities," he said. "Do you know how to steer a boat?"

Mohammad shook his head.

Heath glanced around at the other children. "Anyone here can steer a boat?"

They shook their heads.

Damn. "Imam, Maryam, come here." They were the oldest and most coherent of the children. He glanced out the window to see the naval vessel almost on them. "This is a compass. You want to make sure the needle is always pointed here." He made a mark with his pen. "The throttle is here. Forward is to accelerate, backwards is to go in reverse and straight up is neutral, which means you won't go anywhere."

The girls and Mohammad nodded.

"Why are you showing them?" Zoe asked. "What do you think is going to happen?"

He grimaced. "Making Plan C. Just in case."

He couldn't hide. The container ship crew had seen him. The Iranians would be looking for him. Even if he hid in one of the under-seat compartments, they would find him. If he slid into the water, he might evade capture, but there was a chance he'd lose his grip and get stuck in the middle of the gulf.

Nope. The best chance was to hope they didn't run his photo through any databases. He was known by a different name in Iran. "Do you still have your phone?" he asked Zoe.

She nodded, tapping her pocket.

"Can you hide it in your underwear?" She was wearing layers of clothing but would likely be searched. Hopefully not thoroughly.

Though her frown deepened, she grabbed her phone out and then hesitated, one hand going to her chest, before she untied her pants and slid the phone into her underwear.

Of course. She already had the cable ties and powder in her bra.

"Tell them the truth." He slid his passport into his shoe.

Outside the navy hailed them in Farsi.

They were still some distance from Qatari waters. He turned to the kids. "The Iranian navy will stop us but hopefully let us continue to Qatar."

Mohammad frowned at him.

"We're still in Iranian waters," Heath told him.

The boy nodded.

"Don't panic," he told the children. "Tell them what happened to you." He placed his hand on the throttle and slowed them. "Whatever happens," he murmured to Zoe. "I will see you and the children get safely home."

"You're frightening me, Heath." She glanced out the window as the border patrol came up alongside them. "What did you do?"

"I can't tell you that. Don't worry. If they call the Australian government, we should be fine." Unless the Iranian government was holding a grudge about Australia deporting their ambassador.

Bad timing. "And call me Darius."

Two men boarded the lifeboat armed with guns and approached the door.

Heath stiffened as he recognised the tall man at the back with a scar under his right eye.

What the hell was Kamran still doing working for the Iranian navy? He should be in prison for what he'd done.

He cursed.
Right now that didn't matter.
He was screwed.

Chapter 8

Heart pounding, he pulled up the scarf he'd used to block the dust, so it covered most of his face. It wouldn't last as a disguise for long, but hopefully long enough to get the drop on Kamran.

"Change of plan. Get the kids to the back of the boat," he murmured to Zoe, passing her his backpack. "I'm a mercenary you hired to help rescue the children. Nisha put you in touch with me. You don't know anything else."

"What—"

"I know the scarred man," Heath said, moving towards the door. "He can't know I'm Australian military." Heath still had his handgun, but shooting naval officials wouldn't end well for anyone. He waited a beat until Zoe started gesturing to the children and then called out in Arabic, "We're unarmed."

He held his hands high so they could see them. "I have twelve children and a woman on board with me."

The first guard, a stocky man, called in Farsi, "Step back from the door."

Heath didn't move. He needed to pretend he didn't understand the language. And give Zoe time to get the children as far away as she could.

"Step back," the man called again in Arabic.

Options ran through his mind, but all of them posed too great a risk to Zoe and the children. If the guards opened fire, it would be a bloodbath.

Heath stepped back and the door opened, both guards rushing in, weapons up, ready to shoot. A couple of girls shrieked, and two of the boys, who were still confused, shrank away from them. Zoe stood between the children and Heath, her legs wide, hands slightly out as if she could shield them from what was about to come.

A protector.

His admiration for her grew.

"Who are you? What are you doing here?" the same man demanded.

Heath kept his hands raised and resisted the urge to look at Kamran, who would shoot with the slightest provocation. "These children were being trafficked aboard the container ship."

The man frowned as if he didn't quite understand, but Kamran repeated it in Farsi and the man nodded. "Who are you?"

"I was hired by this woman to rescue them." He gestured to Zoe. "Zoe Yelton is part of the Australian embassy staff."

A flash of concern crossed the man's face as he realised the political implications. "Why did you steal the lifeboat?" The man kept his distance, pointing his gun at Heath, while Kamran moved to the other end of the lifeboat to watch the children.

Heath shifted so he could keep Kamran in his peripheral vision. "Zoe discovered the children had been loaded onto the ship. I hoped we would get them off before the ship departed, but we weren't able to as they had all been drugged." He gestured to the two groggiest boys.

"Why not ask the captain to help?"

"We didn't know who was involved. I thought it would be easier to take the lifeboat and return the children to their parents in Qatar." He gestured in that direction. "Which is why we are heading that way. We didn't mean to enter Iranian waters."

The man kept his guard up, and on the other side of the boat, Kamran was relaying Zoe's name to the crew on the boat. It might take some time to corroborate their story, even if Dobby had contacted Arash.

"Full name," Kamran demanded.

"Darius Darvish," Heath replied. At least Kamran was on the boat with him and wouldn't see the associated photo.

"They rescued us," Mohammad yelled. "We want to go home."

Kamran glanced at him but repeated the name into the radio.

"Running it now," came the voice in Farsi.

The hairs stood up on Heath's arms. Fuck. He knew that voice. Another man who should be in prison, but due to his contacts had merely been demoted. He should have suspected Ali would be around if Kamran was here. Ali had never gone anywhere without his chief enforcer.

What were the chances?

Pretty fucking small.

He'd definitely jinxed the mission by saying it was going to be simple.

The second Ali saw Heath's ID photo, the shit was going to hit the fan.

The guard nearest to him had lowered his gun enough that Heath could disarm him, but Kamran was a shoot first, ask questions later kind of man, and if Heath was injured, he couldn't protect Zoe.

He was running out of time.

"Excuse me."

Heath's gaze whipped to Zoe as she touched

Kamran's arm. What the hell was she doing? Kamran turned to her and away from Heath.

"The children are scared…"

Heath tuned out the rest of her words as he attacked the guard closest to him, disarming him and knocking him unconscious.

Heath brought up the gun and pointed it at Kamran as Kamran grabbed Zoe and hauled her against him as a shield.

He itched to shoot the man who had caused devastation and fear to so many people, but to do so would cause an even greater international incident.

"Drop it," Kamran barked. Over the radio came Ali's voice. "Darius is Navid Ismail!"

Kamran grinned and tightened his hold on Zoe. She winced, staring at Heath with a healthy dose of fear, but also so much trust in her eyes.

He didn't deserve it.

"You want me to put a bullet into her?" Kamran asked in Farsi. "You know I'm untouchable."

Heath's gut roiled. He kept the gun steady on Kamran as options came to him and were discarded.

The problem was Kamran was right. No matter what he and Ali did, they weren't punished for it. He would shoot Zoe, and then

Heath, and then sink the lifeboat with all the children so there were no witnesses.

But if it was revenge he wanted, he would keep Heath alive long enough to torture him, and the longer he lived, the more time he had to escape.

There was always a slim possibility one or more of the other men on the vessel weren't completely in Ali's pockets or had a conscience.

"You've got five seconds, Navid."

Which was more like three the way Kamran worked. Heath slowly lowered the gun. "I see you're still Ali's guard dog, Kamran."

Anger crossed Kamran's face. "Drop it," he snarled.

The other guard was coming around, and the children were staring at him wide-eyed with fear.

He placed the weapon on the seat next to him, away from the guard.

Outside, Ali rushed to the side of the naval vessel, weapon in hand. Time hadn't made him any less angry.

"Darius?" Zoe asked.

She'd remembered his cover name. "Everything will be fine," he told her.

The guard he hit got to his feet a little unsteadily. "Hold out your hands."

Heath did as he was asked and the guard

slapped handcuffs onto him and then searched him, finding and removing the handgun. Maybe he could convince Kamran and Ali to let the others go. They were innocent.

"They should let you go with the kids. Contact Dobby. Tell him I'm with Ali."

Zoe's hand clenched, hiding the phone number, and she nodded.

"Out," Kamran demanded and gestured with his gun. He still held Zoe, but any demands Heath tried to make would backfire. Kamran always loved to make things difficult for him.

Heath stepped into the doorway and up the stairs. The waves rocked the boat and the wind buffeted him. In the far distance, the dust storm coloured the horizon, but the smell didn't carry on the wind.

Ali's angry glare morphed into triumph.

Behind him, the guard he'd disarmed picked up his weapon. "What about the others?"

"Bring them all onto the boat," Ali responded.

***

Zoe couldn't follow the barked commands in Farsi, but what she did understand was things weren't going well. Heath was in handcuffs and being removed from the boat, and she still had a gun pressed against her side.

"Please!" Zoe begged, and Kamran focused

on her. "Let us go. These children have been through enough trauma."

The man ignored her, watching until Heath was on the other boat, and then spoke into his radio and released his hold on her.

He received a response and glanced at them. "On your feet. Follow him."

Zoe hesitated. While she didn't want to leave Heath on his own, she also had to consider the safety of the children she'd rescued.

"Now!"

"They need help," she said in Arabic. "They were drugged. They're still unsteady."

"Help them, then."

No. She couldn't let them get on the other boat. There was no way the Iranians would drop the children in Qatar before returning home. Tensions were already strained in the area, and an Iranian vessel entering Qatari waters without permission, particularly with the uprising going on, wouldn't be taken lightly. She glanced outside to where a gleeful Iranian commander was shoving Heath to the ground. He must be Ali, and from the patches on the uniform he looked like he was in charge.

He could do what he liked.

But perhaps he was the type who would want the easy route.

She took a few steps to the open door and

called, "None of these children have identification."

Ali glanced at her.

"Do you want to be stuck with the nightmare of dealing with a dozen children who were born in Pakistan but are living in Qatar and have no way of contacting their families because communications are down in the country?"

The man frowned.

"Will your government appreciate the cost of accommodation, food and then flights to get them home again?"

Real concern crossed his face. The boats rocked, and Zoe braced herself against the door frame as she waited for his response.

Finally he barked an order in Farsi. Zoe glanced at Heath for a translation.

"They're letting you and the children go. They only want me."

Fear filled her. What would they do to him? Heath had risked his life because of her. She couldn't leave him to be arrested.

"It's OK, Zoe. Dobby will get you out of Qatar. Stay with Nisha."

She shook her head. He thought she was worried about herself. "I don't care about that. I care about what happens to you." It was her fault they were in this mess. "I'm so sorry. I keep thinking I know what's best, keep defying orders.”

“Don’t doubt your instincts,” Heath said. “They’re spot on.”

A little relief filled her but it didn’t help their situation.

Ali grinned and spoke in English. “You two seem close. I’d better not separate you.” He shouted an order to Kamran.

“Leave her,” Heath said. “Those children don’t know how to drive a lifeboat. They’re too young to be left alone.”

Ali peered through the boat’s windows. “There’re enough of them. Show them which way to go. They will be fine.”

Shit. This wasn’t good. She glanced back at the children. Maryam’s eyes were wide. “What’s happening?”

“He’s under arrest.”

“Why?”

“I don’t know.”

“What’s going to happen to us?” Mohammad asked.

“They’re going to let you continue to Qatar,” she explained.

“What about you?” Imam asked.

“Ali, they’re children,” Heath argued. “They can’t be left alone. Let her go with them. You’ve got me.”

“Yes, but if I’ve got her, I’ve got leverage over

you." Ali sounded positively gleeful.

This wasn't an ordinary arrest. This was a man with a grudge against Heath. Zoe's chest tightened. She was in a tug-of-war. She'd started this to see the children safely home, but she couldn't abandon the man who had helped her so much.

She might not have a choice.

"Show them how to drive the boat," Ali demanded.

This was why Heath had given them instructions. Planning for different contingencies. The guard pulled her away from the door, and Zoe walked to the steering wheel where she gestured to Imam, Maryam and Mohammad.

The boat rocked side to side and the motion was unsettling. She placed a hand on her stomach and Imam looked pale. It wouldn't be so bad after they started moving again.

Everything around the steering wheel was clearly labelled in English.

She repeated Heath's instructions. "When you get to the Qatari coast, you should recognise the port when it comes into view." Would the Americans still be there? "There are military men at the entrance. If it is quiet, approach them and say Zoe and Joker sent you. Tell them what happened. They might be able to help." She just hoped whatever disturbance had caused them to rush back to the entrance was over. "If there's shooting, stay in the boat until it's quiet. There's plenty of food and water under the seats."

Mohammad nodded, looking a little scared but determined.

"When you get to Nisha, ask her to call me when the telephones are back on. She has my number." And hopefully Zoe would still have her phone.

"I don't feel well," Iman said. She placed a hand on her stomach, and her face was pale.

Zoe glanced around for a bag. "I think she's going to be sick," she said to Kamran.

Imam pushed past him and leaned against the door frame, vomiting towards the other boat. Ali leapt away from the edge, as Iman emptied the meagre contents of her stomach.

Ali shouted something to the remaining guard on the lifeboat and then called someone else to take Heath away.

Heath nodded at her, his eyes full of the promise that he would get them out of this. She exhaled. This was her fault. She would have to fix it.

She scanned the boat, noting another pair of guards with Heath and two more in the wheelhouse. Eight men.

Zoe rubbed Imam's back as the girl continued to retch. "It won't be so bad when the boat is moving." Hopefully.

"Hurry up," the guard said in Arabic. "You need to get moving."

Mohammad appeared with a sick bag he must have found in the supplies. He handed it to Imam, and Zoe helped her back inside to a seat.

She glanced at the children. All were conscious now, but only a few seemed to realise their predicament. "Do you understand what you need to do?" she asked Maryam and Mohammad.

Maryam repeated her instructions and then asked, "Will you be all right?"

Zoe nodded. "Of course. We'll get this misunderstanding sorted out in no time." She smiled with a lot more optimism than she felt. "Take care, and pay attention to the compass and anything outside you could hit; boats, reefs, rocks. Anything under water might have waves and white water over it, so go around." There weren't too many cargo ships within sight, but that could change. She hugged Maryam and Mohammad. "You'll be fine. Your parents will be so excited to see you." She picked up Heath's backpack and swung it over one shoulder, beside her own.

Ali shouted something from outside, and the guard grabbed her arm, his grip painful, and pulled her towards the door.

Maryam and Mohammad watched her go with fear and determination on their faces. Zoe exhaled. They would be all right. She had to believe it. These lifeboats were made for survival and as long as they kept heading in the right direction, they would reach land in a few hours.

Carefully she climbed between the boats, stumbling as the waves bumped them both. By the time she righted herself, Kamran was on the navy boat behind her and he threw the painter line of the lifeboat into the water, casting it adrift.

Immediately it moved forward, heading for home.

The children were on their own.

There was nowhere she and Heath could run to, no way to escape. Zoe adjusted her hijab to make sure she was presentable, while also scanning the deck to spot a life raft on this boat.

There was a small capsule at the back, but there were also eight armed sailors to avoid.

Out of the frying pan and into the fire. The boat moved, turning slowly to point in the direction it had come from, and accelerated. Heading towards Iran. She stumbled again, still getting used to the movement.

She was ushered into an empty cabin which had seating around a table. "Where's Darius?" she asked Kamran, who had accompanied her inside.

"Talking to the commander." He patted her down, his hands lingering over her breasts. Instantly her knee came up and hit him square in the groin. He groaned and backhanded her, knocking her down onto the seat.

Her cheek stung and tears welled in her eyes as she met his angry gaze. "Sorry, instinct. I tend to do that when a man touches me without warning."

He glowered and said something to the two other guards who came into the cabin. Then he left the room.

Zoe exhaled. He was mean and had a history with Heath.

Another sailor, this one younger and a little nervous, his eyes not meeting hers, approached her. "We need to search you," he said in broken Arabic.

She nodded and stood with her arms outstretched and legs spread. Cautiously he patted her down, finding the multi-tool Heath had given her, but avoiding her breasts. The cable ties and sleeping powder were safe.

The other guard took both backpacks and searched them. He said something to the young one who asked, "What's this?"

The guard held an array of equipment, including binoculars and rope, as well as food.

"Supplies," Zoe said. "We didn't know what we would need to save the children. Please, may I try to contact their parents? They'll be very worried."

"No calls," Kamran said as he returned. "Commander wants to question you next." He grinned as if relishing the thought.

Fear spiked in Zoe.

"Sit." Kamran pointed and Zoe sank into the hard seat. Time to take stock and come up with Plan D.

It was almost dark now, with the last rays of the sun just sinking below the horizon. She didn't know how to navigate by the stars, and the moon hadn't appeared yet.

The idea of being stuck in a foreign country when no one knew where she was terrified her

No, Heath's team knew the Iranian navy had been approaching them. It would give them a place to start looking. And she still had her phone with GPS.

They couldn't just disappear.

The Australian embassy in Iran had been in Tehran, on the opposite side of the country, but had recently been closed with the relationships between countries in the Middle East deteriorating.

And there'd been that incident when Australia had kicked the Iranian ambassador out of the country, so the government might not feel too friendly to Australians at the moment.

The closest embassy now was in the UAE, and they were heading in the wrong direction.

Assuming they were being taken to the Iranian coast, the nearest country by road would be Pakistan or Afghanistan, and the closest country by sea would be Oman. An option because relations between Australia and Oman were good.

But they would need to steal a boat, and one fast enough to outrun the one they were currently on.

Who was she kidding? She didn't have the slightest clue how they would get out of this. She didn't even know what Heath had done to cause his arrest. She sighed and slumped into the chair, exhaustion hitting her.

Something pricked the underside of her breast.

Cable ties.

And with them was the sleeping powder. Could she drug these men? She doubted she'd have enough for eight, but if she could drug those watching her, she could get away, and maybe rescue Heath. Then he could do his thing with the rest of them.

But she needed them to think she was harmless.

Zoe relaxed her clenched hand and noticed Dobby's number written on it. Perhaps he could give her some tips if she could call him.

She repeated Dobby's phone number over again in her head while she studied the guards.

Kamran would be the hardest. The youngest couldn't have been long out of high school and was staring out the window, looking bored, and the other was looking uncomfortable having her there.

Maybe he didn't agree with what Ali was doing. He could be an ally.

Should she demand to see Heath, or would that make Kamran think they were closer than they were?

Too many questions and no answers.

Zoe closed her eyes and started reviewing options.

Chapter 9

At a loud thud, Zoe's eyes flashed open. The young sailor stood over her, and on the table was a cup of water. She glanced at him.

"Drink." He was the only one in the room.

Zoe reached for the cup, her mouth dry. How long had she been sitting with her eyes closed? Surely it wasn't too long.

The cable ties in her bra pricked her, reminding her of the sleeping powder nestled in her cleavage. Had they spiked this drink?

She hadn't been handcuffed, but that didn't mean they weren't treating her as a suspect. "Where's Darius?" she asked in Arabic.

"Busy with the commander."

She adjusted her hijab, tucking back some loose hair, and swallowed hard. Across on the window ledge was her multi-tool, and below it were their backpacks. Too far away to reach.

"Where are we going? May I call my boss? He'll be worried." She checked the time. Just over half an hour since they'd spoken to Dobby.

The sailor glanced behind her and she turned to find another guard at the entrance to the deck.

"Back to Iran," he said. "After we make a stop." His English was stilted, but she appreciated he knew some.

"Where?" There weren't many islands, and it wasn't likely an Iranian naval vessel would go into UAE or Oman waters. She glanced out at the night but had no idea which direction they were travelling.

The sailor didn't answer.

Would it give them an opportunity to escape? She needed to act fast. "May I use the bathroom?" It would allow her to call Dobby and see the layout of the boat.

The man grunted and gestured for her to follow the young sailor. They passed a galley kitchen before he showed her to a tiny cubicle with a toilet in it. She closed the door and retrieved her phone from her underwear. No reception.

Damn it.

Still, if she typed out a text, it might send when she did get reception. Quickly she typed a text to Dobby, telling him they were on the Iranian vessel, that Heath knew the commander, Ali, and they were making a stop somewhere before heading back to Iran. She saved the contact into her phone, used the toilet, and then pulled up her pants and replaced the phone.

After washing her hands, she used the tap to drink some water. She was worried about being drugged, but perhaps the sailors wouldn't have the same concerns about her. If she could ask for a cup of tea… offer to make them one too.

It was worth a shot.

She retrieved the plastic bag of sleeping powder and slipped it into her pocket. Hopefully they wouldn't search her again.

The guard pounded on the door, and she opened it with an apologetic smile. "Thank you."

On the way back to the room, they passed the kitchen. She stopped and the sailor almost bumped into her. "May I make some tea?"

She didn't wait for his response, simply entered the room and reached for the kettle. "Would you like one?"

He glanced at her with concern and confusion, but she smiled, filling the kettle and put it on to boil as if she did it every day.

"Do you have any cups?" She cupped her hands in case he didn't understand, and he pointed to the cupboard above her. She held up two and smiled. "Yes?"

He nodded, relaxing a little, and she got a third one down for the older guard who might still be in the main room.

Could she get the sleeping powder into the tea without him seeing? Unlikely since he was less than a metre away.

She didn't even know how much she should use or how quickly it would work.

Drugging government officials would probably land her in an Iranian gaol.

But who knew what they were doing with Heath?

If they'd resolved matters, surely they'd reunite them.

Exhaling a shaky breath, she measured tea leaves into the teapot and added the water. While she waited for it to steep, she placed her hands in her pockets, trying one-handed to rip the packet.

She couldn't do it.

Her heart racing, she poured three cups of tea.

A shout from further inside the boat and the sailor turned, taking a couple of steps out of the room into the corridor, his hand going to the gun on his hip.

Was that Heath?

She couldn't tell whether it was a shout of pain or anger, but she needed to act fast.

Pulse pounding, Zoe ripped the packet and poured half of it into two of the cups and tucked the plastic into her pocket just as the sailor turned back. She glanced at him. "Do you like sugar cubes with your tea?"

He held up two fingers.

Zoe placed two sugar cubes in the cup and stirred. The powder dissolved and she stirred the other cup as well. "Your friend?" She pointed to the cup and held up the cubes. He shook his head.

Right. At least the tea looked normal and not milky.

She handed him his drink and picked up the other two, making note of the drugged one. "Shall we go?"

She followed the sailor out of the galley and through the room she'd been sitting in. Zoe handed the older guard his tea and sat opposite him, facing the door out to the deck. It was closed now, maybe to keep the cold night air out. She held her breath as he took his first sip, but he said nothing about the taste.

What was she going to do with them if the drug did work? They each had handcuffs on their belts, and she could gag them with her hijab, but if any of the other men came into the room, they would raise the alarm.

She could take their guns, but she had no idea how to fire one. Did they have safety things she had to switch off?

Better to take them anyway. They would still

have their machine guns which lined the wall of the room, but maybe she could hide them in the toilet or something. She would have to find Heath and hope she could free him.

She sipped her tea. How long would it take to work?

What if the other guards came into the room before it had taken effect?

Her pulse felt as if it was going to vibrate right out of her skin.

The older guard finished his tea and placed the empty cup on the table. He said something to the younger one and left the room. A few moments later she heard the sound of a door closing.

Maybe going to the bathroom.

The younger guard drank more tea and watched her with curiosity.

She took another small sip of her tea, and he drank some of his. "May I call someone?" she asked again. "So they know I am safe."

"No. The Commander must approve." He finished his drink.

There was little chance of that happening.

Down the corridor there was a thud, and they both turned, the guard getting to his feet, his hand pulling out his gun. He called something in Farsi.

No answer.

He glanced towards the deck and then at her. "Stay there." He moved towards the corridor.

Zoe glanced at the windowsill. Her multi-tool and the backpacks still sat there. She shifted to the edge of her seat. The guard glanced back at her and then focused ahead. He called out a name.

Maybe the tea had worked.

Carefully, keeping her eye on the young guard, she stood and tiptoed to the windowsill, picking up her multi-tool and slipping it into her pocket.

Another thud.

She moved back into the corridor to find the young guard lying on the ground.

Shit. It had worked. She stared in disbelief for a moment before a groan deeper into the boat made her move. She rushed to the deck door and locked it, noting two men on the deck looking out at the ocean.

Zoe grabbed both backpacks and then ran to check the guard. He was still breathing. She shifted the gun away from him and found his handcuffs, quickly cuffing his hands behind his back. She grabbed the key to the cuffs and then tried to drag him into the galley, but he was too heavy.

It would take too much time, and Kamran could reappear at any moment.

She left him there and continued into the cabin.

The other guard was just outside the toilet. She took his gun and cuffed him as well.

Cautiously she picked up the second gun. It felt heavy and unfamiliar in her hands, a weapon she didn't know how to control.

But no one else knew that.

She braced herself and headed deeper into the boat. Heath had to be somewhere with the two men who hated him.

She had to find him.

***

The room Ali pushed Heath into was clearly meant to hold prisoners. Grey metal walls and a cramped space in the hull of the boat, with rings on the wall to tie people to and a very thick, solid door as the only entrance and exit. Heath braced his feet to account for the rock of the boat and watched Ali.

The man had been unpredictable when Heath worked for him as part of an undercover intelligence mission. He was the type of man who revelled in his power and exerting it over others. Heath had avoided his wrath by being good at his job and keeping a low profile. He'd spent six months earning Ali's trust and figuring out just how narcotics were being passed through Iran and into Australia. The resulting sting had closed down that avenue permanently, but he had been marked as a wanted man.

The fact that Ali had avoided going to prison meant he must have a lot of dirt on some very powerful people. The naval coast guard was the absolute worst place for someone who had been involved in drug smuggling.

Or, the very best place if they wanted him to continue his activities.

Something to consider. There might be drugs on the boat right now.

Heath hadn't missed the respect on the other sailors' faces as Ali had handcuffed him. That probably meant Ali had convinced them to follow him into whatever scheme he was running now. He always had a silver tongue.

That meant Heath would get no support from any of the other men he'd spotted on the boat. Each man held a machine gun, handgun and, Heath guessed, several knives. His chances of being able to sneak around and disarm them all without raising alarm weren't zero, but they also weren't high. If Zoe wasn't on the boat, he would have tried it, but she was a bargaining chip he wouldn't gamble with.

He hoped the cargo ship's captain had reported the incident in his logbook and his call for help would have been broadcast across the airways.

Not that records couldn't be changed.

"I knew one day I would get my revenge," Ali said, speaking in Farsi.

Heath stayed silent. It didn't matter what he said now. Ali was looking for an excuse to hit him.

Kamran entered the room. "That woman of yours is feisty." He grinned. "It will be fun to teach her some respect."

Heath fought to keep his expression neutral. "She's not my woman."

"You always did have a soft spot for women and children in need," Ali said. "A quirk I allowed because you were a good soldier."

Kamran scowled. He'd always hated Heath due to the way Ali had accepted him so readily into the team.

"But," Ali continued, "perhaps they will be your undoing now. We'd be quite within our rights to shoot that lifeboat out of the water." He grinned. "Stolen and entering Iranian waters, running from the authorities." He left the words hanging.

Heath stared back at him, his gut tight. It wasn't an idle threat. It was just the kind of thing Ali would do to make sure there were no witnesses to what he'd done.

The boat had to be close to Qatari waters now if the kids had put it into full throttle. Would he risk the international incident, or was Ali banking on the fact the Qatari government had their hands full dealing with the revolt?

"So calm," Ali said. "I always admired your even temper. A good asset."

"A traitor," Kamran reminded him.

Ali nodded. "How much did they pay you to betray me?"

Interesting. Ali hadn't discovered his true identity. "They told me Kamran was ready to talk and they could only keep one of us out of gaol." Heath shrugged. "I liked my freedom."

Ali glanced at Kamran and raised his eyebrows.

"He's lying. No one approached me."

"Then they lied to me. I should have guessed." He smiled. "It was just business." Words Ali had said on multiple occasions to people he had betrayed.

Ali nodded. "As is this." He nodded to Kamran who took two quick steps towards Heath and punched him in the face.

Darkness.

Chapter 10

Cold water shocked Heath awake and he blinked rapidly, trying to bring a hand up to clear his vision, only to find they were cuffed above him and connected to a ring in the ceiling. His face throbbed, and as his eyes cleared, he found both Kamran and Ali smiling at him.

Shit.

"Cheap shot," he said, knowing it would irritate Kamran. He braced himself for the gut punch and breathed out through the pain, though his bullet-proof vest cushioned some of the blow.

Kamran frowned and clenched his hand around his fist. Probably hurt him as much as it hurt Heath.

"You were never willing to go head to head with me because you knew you'd lose. But now you've got me at a slight disadvantage…"

The next two punches knocked the air out of his lungs, but at least Kamran was staying away from his head.

He needed to keep them focused on him so they didn't think about Zoe. Heath just hoped the other sailors weren't like these two and hadn't been instructed to interrogate her.

The thought that they could be hurting Zoe made him straighten and bite his tongue against taunting Kamran again. He looked at Ali. "What's the plan?" He stretched his fingers up and felt the chain above him.

"I had considered throwing you into the ocean and pretending we'd never seen you," Ali said. "But you have an annoying resilience and would likely survive."

There was a measure of respect in Ali's voice. Kamran heard it as well and scowled, punching Heath again.

"There's also a chance Zoe's government might be able to trace you back to the cargo ship and the captain will tell them we came after you."

"International politics can be tricky," Heath agreed. He waited, knowing there was more to come. Ali wouldn't, couldn't, let him go unpunished. It went against his whole ethos.

Another punch, this time very close to his ribs. He'd never been sympathetic to a punching bag before now. He was going to hurt tomorrow despite the vest.

Assuming he survived the night.

"I have some friends we're meeting," Ali continued. "They were annoyed when you put an end to our trade." He smiled. "And fortunately they don't care about politics."

His mind whirled. Drug smugglers in the Gulf could belong to any nation. He'd heard rumours pirates were getting bolder about coming in and robbing boats as well.

The cargo ship had been putting up barbed wire.

Zoe was definitely in danger. He had to get free before that happened. Movement at the door made him glance that way. Zoe peeked into the room then disappeared.

How the hell had she got free?

Perhaps no one thought to guard her.

He shifted his gaze to Ali. "So you're leaving the dirty work to someone else?"

"As much as I don't want to, it seems convenient this time."

Both men were watching him and didn't see Zoe step into the room and raise a handgun, gripping it with both hands. Her arms shook, but the determination on her face made his heart thump.

No, she shouldn't be in here. His pulse hammered in his chest. There was no way to tell her to go without bringing attention to her.

Kamran would shoot her.

These people were not reasonable.

"Let him go." Her voice was loud, but he heard the tremor. Shit.

Both men whirled around to face her. "What the hell?" Ali exclaimed. "Where are my men?"

"Indisposed," Zoe replied, her gaze not moving from them. "Uncuff Darius now."

She wore her backpack and even remembered the name he'd given. The pride he felt clashed with his terror for her.

"Now, don't be too hasty." Ali's hand dipped towards the gun on his waist.

"Keep your hands up." She lowered the gun to point at his groin. "Or I will shoot."

Heath gripped the chain above him as Kamran shifted to the side so he wasn't directly behind Ali. The movement brought him close enough to Heath.

Heath struck, lifting himself up and wrapping his legs around Kamran's neck. He squeezed hard, cutting off his windpipe until the man slumped to the ground.

Zoe flinched, but kept the gun on Ali. "Take the cuffs off him."

Ali hadn't even turned to see what had happened behind him. "No."

"I will shoot you."

The arsehole shook his head. "If you do that, my whole crew will be down here in a matter of seconds.”

Zoe hesitated.

“They won’t hear over the sound of the engine,” Heath told her.

She glanced at Heath, and Ali lunged at her. Zoe pulled the trigger. The noise exploded around the metal room, making Heath’s ears ring.

Zoe jerked back, her body not expecting the recoil, and stumbled out of Ali’s reach. The man fell to the ground, roaring in pain.

Zoe stared at Ali, her hands trembling, but the rest of her was frozen.

“Zoe!” Heath called. If Ali wasn’t badly injured, he would be after her in seconds.

She didn’t move.

“Zoe. Look at me.” He struggled with the cuffs, trying to get them loose.

She looked up and blinked, coming back to her senses. She dashed past a still groaning Ali and fished handcuff keys out of her pocket, stretching up to unlock his cuffs.

She smelled like dust, salt air, and hope.

Heath kept his gaze on Ali as the man rolled over, his leg covered in blood. The cuffs clicked open and Heath jerked his hands down, grabbing the gun from Zoe’s hand and pushing her behind him, just as Ali found his own gun.

Two bullets made the gun fall from Ali’s hand

and neutralised him. Zoe jumped. "Don't look at him," Heath said as he turned to her. "Keep your eyes on the doorway. I need to restrain Kamran. How did you get away?" He kept his voice calm, and she fixed her eyes on the doorway, her face pale.

"I drugged the two guards with the powder you gave me."

Clever girl. He'd get the details later, but now he tied Kamran to the same shackles that had held him and stripped both bodies of their weapons, tucking the second gun into the back of his pants. The engine noise shifted, slowing.

Shit. Had they heard the gunshots?

He grabbed Zoe's hand and pulled her past Ali and into the corridor. Her hand trembled in his, but she followed him, pausing just long enough to grab his backpack and hand it to him.

"Two guards on the deck and I think two guards in the wheelhouse," she said. "The two I drugged were too heavy to hide and I don't know how long the powder lasts."

"They'll be out for at least an hour." Heath turned down another corridor to where there was a hatch to the deck.

Quickly he climbed it and pried it open, peering out. Darkness on one side of the deck, but a bright spotlight on the other where a fancy luxury boat was approaching.

Shit. They must be the smugglers. He lowered the hatch. There was a small nook just next to it where rope was coiled, but it was big enough for Zoe to hide in.

"Backpack." She wouldn't fit with it on.

"What's happening?"

"Another boat is approaching—smugglers. We don't want those men to get aboard. They'll want to see Ali."

She paled further, handing him the backpack with shaking hands.

"I need you to hide in there." He pointed at the small space.

Her face grew paler still, but she nodded and climbed in.

He hated to do that to her again. "It won't be for long." He squeezed her hand. "Don't get out for any reason until I come get you. There might be a lot of shooting and I don't want you hit."

He helped her in, brushed a thumb over her cheek, the motion as natural as breathing. "I'll be back as soon as I can."

Heath checked the deck. Two guards were standing on the deck illuminated by the spotlight, waiting for the boat which was still a hundred metres out. He climbed out.

Another sailor was climbing down from the wheelhouse, looking annoyed.

Heath moved through the shadows and

waited at the bottom of the ladder. The second the man was in reach, Heath grabbed him and knocked him out, dragging him into the shadows and restraining him with cable ties. He threw the man's weapons overboard and glanced at the wheelhouse. The boat was slowing further. He had to make sure the smugglers didn't board.

He had little time to overpower the other two guards and get up to the wheelhouse before the boat would be alongside. And the smugglers would have firepower of their own.

He exhaled and shot the spotlight so the world went dark.

The captain accelerated, probably thinking the smugglers were shooting at them. Heath grabbed the ladder to steady himself and then rushed the two guards who had taken cover and weren't expecting an attack from behind. He knocked one out, and then the other, and quickly restrained them while the boat continued to accelerate.

That should be everyone on deck taken care of. He climbed the ladder, reaching the wheelhouse platform.

Heath waited a couple of beats and peered inside, spotting just the one man, surrounded by glowing panels. He glanced towards the smugglers and called Ali on the radio.

Suddenly light flooded the area as the smugglers' boat turned on its floodlights. Inside, the captain shaded his eyes, and the radio sounded a warning about a man outside.

Damn. The smugglers knew something was wrong. Heath rushed in. The captain tried to get his gun up, but Heath was too fast, overpowering him in seconds.

He breathed out while he tied the captain up and handcuffed him to a rail on the far side of the wheelhouse.

Heath glanced outside. The luxury boat was about fifty metres off the port side, not gaining, but not falling behind either. Heath checked the coordinates and the map on the display.

Shit. They were well and truly in Iranian waters now. He shifted the wheel, heading south-east towards Dubai.

The window behind him shattered, and he ducked as military-grade bullets smashed through the cabin.

The smugglers wanted whatever was on board.

He covered his head and hid behind the cupboard on the port side of the boat, the only thing that gave the slightest bit of protection. The steering wheel turned, making the boat lurch.

"You won't get away," the captain said.

"Those men are psychotic."

Good to know. Heath grabbed the rope out of his pocket, spotted something he could tie the wheel to, and after the next burst of fire, he dashed over, corrected their course, and tied the wheel into position.

Up here was a small arsenal of machine guns.

Heath grinned, grabbing one, checking it over and peering over the edge at the boat. Their lights were still on, illuminating all four on deck.

Easy pickings.

He aimed for the captain, gave a short burst of fire from the gun, and ducked down again.

Return fire had more glass shattering around him. He shifted positions, moving along the wall, and waited for the fire to finish and then peered up. The boat had veered off course, and someone was climbing up to correct it. Heath shot him and then spotted a man at the front of the boat with a fucking rocket launcher. Heath swung his weapon and shot. A second later the rocket launched, but straight into the air.

One more to go.

He ducked down as another round of fire came and he shifted again, knowing the light from the machine gun fire would give away his position. Heath checked to make sure the captain was still restrained and found him full of bullet holes.

Shit.

He scanned the luxury boat for movement. The man at the front was dead on the deck and a second later the light disappeared.

The remaining smuggler must have shot it out.

Heath blinked to adjust his eyes and spotted a shadow entering the wheelhouse. Heath aimed, but before he fired, the boat decelerated and fell behind.

Smart man.

Heath waited until the luxury boat peeled away and headed in the opposite direction out of reach before he went back to the steering wheel. The panels were smashed, but they were still heading in the right direction.

Towards Dubai.

He wouldn't get a great reception with two dead men on board and an Iranian naval boat which had been shot to pieces. Which meant he needed a better boat.

He glanced at the luxury boat. Only one hostile on board there, and he had six on this one.

He turned and headed after the boat.

He'd need Zoe to help him. He checked the panels and saw a switch for the deck lights, which he turned on. The three guards he'd disarmed were still tied up, but trying to get free.

He found the hailing device and said, "Zoe, it's safe to come out. Come to the deck."

While he waited for the hatch to open, Heath grabbed his phone and dialled Dobby.

"Sitrep."

"You don't want to know," Heath said. "I'm going to commandeer a smuggler's boat."

Dobby didn't skip a beat. "Zoe and the kids?"

"Safe, I think. The kids are still in the lifeboat heading towards Qatar. Can you contact Rambo and see if they're still in the area? Need someone to pick up the kids."

"Done." Dobby relayed the information to someone else on the plane. "Zoe?"

He glanced at the hatch to find her climbing out. "With me." He was gaining on the smugglers' boat, which hadn't seemed to realise he was coming after it. "Plan to head to the UAE when we're done."

"Flights are at five or seventeen fifteen," Dobby told him.

Heath smiled. The team had been planning contingencies for his extraction. "Copy." He leaned out the broken window and waved to Zoe. "Up here." To Dobby he said, "Will report in when we hit land."

"Copy."

Heath hung up as Zoe appeared at the door,

her face concerned as she stared at the shattered glass and then at him. "Are you all right?" She hurried to him, checking him over. Her hands on his arms and chest were soothing.

"Yeah. I need your help. We're going to get on that boat." He pointed to the luxury boat and picked up the hailing device. "Stop your boat and move to the deck with your hands up." His voice boomed across the water.

Zoe gasped. Heath spun around and found her staring at the dead captain. He took her hand and tugged her towards him. "The smugglers shot him. Don't look."

She tore her eyes away and stared out the window.

He had another spotlight, which he moved to shine on the fleeing smuggler.

The man cringed, but the boat slowed and he climbed down to the deck. "Everyone on board move to the back deck," Heath ordered. He doubted there were more people on board, but it was worth checking. "Zoe, I'm going to pull alongside the boat and get on. You stay here." He handed her one of the handguns he'd collected and she took it reluctantly.

"It's for your protection. I want you to stay here until I've cleared the other boat." He showed her how to brace her hands around the gun. "Everyone is restrained, so this is just in case."

Her dark eyes widened, but she nodded.

"When the boat is clear, I'll bring it alongside and wave you to come over."

"Why not stay here?"

"We've got six hostiles on board and this boat will attract more attention."

"Won't they come after us?"

"It'll take them time to get free, and by then we'll be long gone."

"Are we going after the children?"

Heath shook his head. "Dobby's getting Rambo to organise someone to pick them up. They'll be almost home by now." He glanced at the luxury boat which was floating in the water and slowed the boat, getting the angle right and slowing further until they had almost reached them. He checked his gun then squeezed her hand. "I won't be long."

Her nod was more confident this time. "Be careful."

He grinned. "Always."

Chapter 11

Zoe's hands gripped the gun tightly as Heath shimmied down the ladder and vaulted onto the luxury boat. The gun was warm from Heath's hands, but it felt dangerous. The amount of damage it could do to a person…

She squeezed her eyes closed at the memory of Ali hunched over, blood spilling everywhere.

She'd shot a man.

A man who hadn't hurt her.

A man who had captured and was hurting Heath.

And she still didn't know what Heath had done.

For the first time during this whole debacle, she felt truly alone. Heath was on another boat and as he restrained the man on board, the boats drifted apart.

She exhaled slowly. Now wasn't the time to panic. Not after everything she'd already gone through.

He would be back for her.

He'd promised.

She glanced around the wrecked cabin, her gaze only briefly touching on the dead man on the ground before moving on, her body shuddering. She gritted her teeth against the nausea swirling inside her. He'd just been doing his job.

She wanted off this boat.

The three men on the deck were talking, but she couldn't hear their words. They were planning something, and she didn't want to be on the boat when they came to an agreement.

She scanned the panel, looking for an off button or switch, and spotted a key. She turned it and the hum of the engine stopped. But the lights also went out.

Quickly she turned the key back a click, and the lights came on.

She rolled her shoulders, trying to shake out the tension.

If she had any skill with a gun, she'd go down there and separate the guards, or fire warning shots or something, but she was more likely to kill them by accident.

Her gaze roamed the rest of the deck as Heath disappeared into the cabin of the other boat.

Half of the boat was in shadow and half was brightly lit, which made it difficult to see in the dark areas.

Was that movement?

She stared hard into the shadows, but nothing moved.

Could she shift the spotlight around? Surely there must be some way of doing it from the inside and Heath didn't need the other boat illuminated.

She scanned the console and found a lever which looked like it would do the job. She swung the light away from the luxury boat and towards the shadowy side of the deck and spotted Kamran creeping along the side carrying a machine gun.

He glanced up and grinned.

How the hell had he got free?

Zoe's heart pounded as he ran along the deck towards the ladder. Obviously he'd seen Heath get onto the other boat. Her hand fumbled for the hailer Heath had used and she searched the luxury deck for him, but he wasn't there.

"Darius, I need help." She winced at the loud volume.

Kamran didn't stop. He made a beeline for the ladder and started to climb. Zoe glanced at the other boat but still didn't see Heath.

She swallowed hard, shifted out of the direct line of the doorway and took cover next to the cupboard. She kneeled in place, hands braced around the gun like Heath had shown her, and waited for the man to enter the room.

The light tap, tap, tap of hands and feet on the metal ladder were like drumbeats issuing a war challenge.

What if Heath had run into more enemies on the other boat?

What if he hadn't heard her call?

Was she going to have to shoot someone else?

Her stomach heaved at the thought, but she swallowed it down.

The door handle squeaked as it turned.

Bang!

Zoe flinched at the noise and the resulting thud that followed.

"Zoe!" Heath's voice.

Her pulse still vibrating, she peered up out of the window. Heath gestured her down.

She waved to show she understood and carefully got to her feet, moving over to the door to check the scarred man's location.

He lay at the bottom of the ladder, his head a mess of blood and brains. Obliterated. Horror rose up, and she stumbled away and vomited the contents of her stomach, tears leaking out of her eyes.

She'd never seen anything like it. The movies always made it seem cleaner, a bullet hole in the front of the head. They never showed what the back of the head looked like.

Though her stomach continued to heave, she had to move, had to get off this boat.

She checked the other guards on deck. They were staring towards the base of the ladder.

Reconsidering any plans they might have had.

She checked on Heath, who was now behind the steering wheel and bringing the luxury boat alongside.

Time to get out of this nightmare.

On her final sweep of the cabin, she spotted the key still in the console and slid it into her pocket, plunging her into darkness, but the lights on the smugglers' boat gave her a guide.

She climbed down the ladder, leaping over where she thought the mess of blood and gore was, and hurried to the opposite side of the boat to where Heath was pulling the boat up.

The smuggler on board lurched to his feet and Zoe stumbled back, but then Heath was there. "Grab the rope." He tossed her the rear rope, and she awkwardly grabbed it.

"We're going to do a swap. Him onto the navy boat and you over here," Heath continued. "Jump over."

With pleasure. She awkwardly climbed onto the deck of the luxury boat, further away from

Heath and the prisoner, and sank to her knees.

Heath supported the man over the side onto the boat because his hands were tied behind his back, retrieved the rope and then hurried to her. "Are you all right?" His hand was warm, but right now she was cold inside.

Still, she nodded. "Can we get away from here?"

"Yeah. Head into the cabin when you're ready. It's clear."

In moments Heath accelerated into the darkness, putting distance between them and the nightmare.

Zoe stayed where she was, curled into a ball as the boat bounced over the waves.

Safe.

She was safe even if those men were dead.

The blood and mess of Kamran's face flashed across her mind, and she blinked rapidly, trying not to heave again.

Had they deserved it?

The thought shocked her, but she took a minute to consider all that had happened since the navy boat had stopped them.

They were doing their jobs, arresting Heath for who knows what he had done.

Was Heath actually the bad guy here?

They had strung him up like they were going to torture him, but that could be standard procedure in Iran.

She hugged herself as she looked up at the cabin. Heath's silhouette was just visible amongst the glow from the dials in the room.

What did she know about him?

He was Australian special forces. But that didn't make him incorruptible.

He was well-prepared.

He had a kind heart to go after the children when his mission was to get the embassy personnel out of Qatar.

But he'd done something to make him a wanted man in Iran. Something that made the men who had arrested him positively gleeful at seeing him.

Then he'd shot them without hesitation.

But he had been protecting her.

She exhaled a shaky breath. Her gut told her he was a good man, but for her own peace of mind she needed confirmation.

Carefully she got to her feet and glanced up. Heath was looking out the window. She waved and pointed to the cabin, hoping he would leave her alone. Someone had to steer the boat, and they weren't far enough away from the navy boat for comfort yet.

He acknowledged her with a wave, and she felt his eyes on her until she passed into the cabin.

She didn't turn on any lights, didn't want to become a spotlight in the dark. But she could make out a few large shapes that indicated a table and bench seats.

She glanced out the window, but the navy boat still bobbed in the water behind them, not moving in any direction.

Zoe sank into a chair and pulled out her phone. A couple of bars. As she unlocked it, she noticed the message she had written earlier had been sent.

There was one person who could answer her questions about Heath.

She dialled Dobby's number.

"Hello?" Part barked greeting, part suspicion.

"Is this Dobby?"

"Who's this?"

Definitely suspicious. "My name is Zoe Yelton—"

"Where's Joker?"

"Steering the boat—"

"What happened?"

She huffed out a breath. "If you stop interrupting me, I'll tell you."

Dobby grunted out what might have been a half-laugh. "Go ahead."

"We were stopped by an Iranian navy patrol," Zoe said. "Heath was arrested by Ali and Kamran. Do you know who they are?"

"Yeah."

"I convinced Ali to let the children continue to Qatar, but he wanted me as leverage." She exhaled. "The boat was attacked by smugglers and we had to shoot a couple of people." She didn't actually know how they factored into the story. She didn't want to mention Heath had shot Iranian navy personnel over the phone in case they recorded these kinds of conversations. "We're now on the smugglers' luxury boat and I think we're heading for the UAE."

"What happened to the smugglers?"

She shuddered. "One of them is on the navy boat. I'm not sure what happened to the rest if there were more." But there were likely to have been a few.

"Did Heath ask you to call me?" Dobby asked.

"No." She hesitated. "I, uh, wanted to ask why Heath was wanted by the Iranian authorities."

"I can't tell you that. It's classified."

A little relief seeped through. "It was part of his role as a special forces soldier?"

A pause. "I can't confirm or deny that."

She bit her lip. It sounded like that was the case, but she still wanted reassurance. "What I'm asking is, was Heath justified in… what he did to escape from the men?"

"Heath would never hurt an innocent." The

words shot out instantly. "He's more likely to get himself injured if it's a choice between them and him." Dobby's tone was gentler now.

Heath had stepped between her and his captor the second he was free.

"You're safe with him," Dobby said. "He will do everything he can to get you back to Australia safely."

Zoe exhaled. "Thank you. I just… after everything that's happened… I wanted to make sure."

"I promise you, you're with one of the best men I know."

Tears welled in relief, and her voice broke. "Thank you."

"You'll be all right, Zoe," Dobby said. "There's a flight home today and you should get there in time. I'll meet you at the airport. Is there anyone you'd like to be there? Any family members?"

"My parents." They'd be so worried. "I don't know how much they know about the situation in Qatar. Don't call them until you know we're on the plane. I don't want them to worry."

"I'll arrange it," Dobby promised.

"Thank you." She hung up and sat in the dark as the boat bumped through the waves. The boat was a decent size, so it should have a couple of bedrooms and a bathroom somewhere.

She headed down a short corridor and felt around for a door. Touching the handle, she opened it and walked into a bedroom. Some light from the sliver of moon was coming through the windows, but she didn't dare turn on the lights. Instead she ran her hands along the wall until she found another door.

Ensuite.

The room was pitch black, so she felt around until she found a light switch. She flicked it, confirmed it was a bathroom, and shut herself inside so the light didn't leak out.

The bathroom was nicer than the one she'd had in her apartment in Qatar. She moved to the sink and stared at her reflection.

Her clothes and face were covered in dust, and there were stains on her clothes. She looked a little pale and if she looked too closely at her abaya, there was also the remains of vomit.

Zoe grimaced. She was a mess.

And there was no way she would get through customs looking like this. She frowned. That was a point. How were they going to get into the UAE without arousing suspicion? They couldn't pull into a harbour with a stolen boat with signs of a gunfight.

What was Heath's plan?

She needed to speak with him, but getting

changed would be nice.

She opened the cupboards and found towels and bathroom supplies, but no clothes. Flicking off the light, she went back into the bedroom and used her phone torch to search the cupboards until she found a suitable top and pants.

It was time to get clean.

***

Zoe had gone into the cabin a few minutes ago, but no lights had come on. Heath fought the urge to check on her. He'd cleared the boat; there was no one else on board. She might not want the bright light to attract attention.

His phone rang and he answered Dobby's call.

"Zoe rang," Dobby said without preamble.

Heath frowned and checked the time. A bit earlier than the two hours he'd told her. "Why?"

"To check your references," Dobby said. "She's scared. Wanted to make sure you weren't going rogue hurting arseholes like Ali."

Heath flinched, then exhaled past the hurt. "Smart. I can't tell her what really went down."

"No," Dobby agreed. "But it would be good to tell her something."

He was right. Heath ran a hand through his hair and winced at the dried blood on his skin.

"I'll talk to her. We're about an hour out from land," he said. "Trying to figure out the best place to arrive so we don't attract much attention." Which meant he had to get cleaned up before they ran into anyone.

He glanced behind, but the naval boat still bobbed in the water, getting further and further behind.

"Embassy wants plausible deniability, so you're on your own on that front."

Heath scowled. "What about Zoe? She's one of them."

"Doesn't matter. You're going to need evidence you arrived through customs so you don't raise concerns when you leave."

Yeah, he'd been thinking about that. "The boat's going to cause questions. There's some damage and blood on board. I don't know where it's registered or to whom."

"Life raft on board?" Dobby asked.

"Yeah." He'd already pretty much settled on what he knew Dobby was going to suggest. "I'll sink the vessel about a kilometre out."

"Copy. Let me know which flight you want and we'll organise it. Zoe wants her parents to meet the plane."

Heath nodded. Made sense she would want them there. He checked the surroundings, but aside from a few container ships in the distance, there wasn't a lot of traffic.

"Talk to Zoe," Dobby said and hung up.

He had to tell her the plan anyway. She wouldn't be keen to be on another lifeboat so soon, and this one didn't have an engine.

Still it was too soon to stop, and he didn't want to tie the steering wheel into position while he went to talk to her in case they ran into something and sank further from land than he wanted to.

He called her phone, but she didn't answer.

Concern skittered across his skin. He had cleared the boat, but perhaps there was a secret compartment for someone to hide in. They would have to smuggle the drugs in somehow.

He tried again just in case she'd put the phone down and hadn't heard it ring.

Nothing.

Shit. He slowed the boat, got his gun and hurried into the cabin, clearing each room until he got to the master bedroom. He opened the door and while it was dark inside, there was a slit of light coming from under the door of the bathroom.

Heath exhaled. "Zoe, are you in there?"

"Yeah. Is everything all right?"

She was probably cleaning up, but he needed to check she wasn't being held hostage. "Can I talk to you?"

She opened the door a crack, her hair wet and a towel wrapped around her waist. "Can you give me a minute?"

Water glistened off her skin, and he had the sudden urge to lick her dry.

Not appropriate.

He moved a little closer so she could see him in the bathroom light and mouthed, *Are you alone*?

She frowned. "What?"

She didn't seem scared, but he spoke quietly. "Are you alone?"

"Why wouldn't I be?"

"I need to check." If she was already worried about her safety, he didn't want to force his way inside.

Frowning, she stepped back, and he quickly cleared the room, checking for any hidden compartments. Zoe was staring at him when he finished.

"This boat is used for smuggling," he said. "There may be hidden compartments. I need to do a more thorough check. Can you get dressed quickly and take over at the helm?"

"Of course."

He stepped out of the bathroom, allowing her to change, and searched the master bedroom.

Clear.

Zoe stepped out, wearing a long dark top and dark pants, her hair still wrapped in a towel.

"Feeling better?"

"A bit. There are more clothes in the cupboard if you want to change."

It was nice of her to think of him. "I will later. First let's get moving again." He led the way back to the helm, showed her the direction they needed to go, and accelerated until they were up to speed. The cabin was remarkably quiet. "I'm going to double-check we're alone and then I'll come back and tell you the plan. If you see anyone on board, you slow down fast, and I'll come up on deck."

She nodded, concern across her face. "Do you think it's likely?"

"No. Everyone would have been called on deck to protect the boat."

"All right."

He gave her what he hoped was a reassuring smile and switched on the deck lights. "You see anything that has you worried, you slow down or call me."

"I will."

Heath made quick work checking the deck and then worked his way down until he reached the engine room. It was noisy as hell, but this was where he would expect to find a compartment. During his time working for Ali, they kept the goods as far away from the common areas as possible.

Sure enough, towards the stern he discovered a large compartment containing two waterproof duffle bags.

Checking the area for wires or any other kind of booby trap, he then lifted them out and took them upstairs away from the noise so he could listen.

From the weight and feel he guessed they were full of money, but he checked them thoroughly before unzipping the first one.

Yep, lots of wads of American dollars.

Drug money.

He did a quick count. Several million dollars. He grabbed two wads of cash in case he needed to bribe someone and to back up his cover story of being a wealthy playboy.

A playboy who wasn't the kind to leave money on a sinking ship.

Then he hesitated as he looked over the amount of money which would set anyone up for life.

The transactions from the money would have caused heartache for families as their loved ones succumbed to their addiction.

Money that made the bad guys richer.

Money that Dobby could use to set up his private security firm to stop the bad guys.

Ethically it was dodgy as fuck, but this wasn't really part of his mission. He should be on a plane heading to Australia right now.

There was no way he could get the money out of the country. Taking it with him would cause more delays and problems if it was discovered.

But if it sank with the ship, it would be useless. Unless it was waterproof, which the bags appeared to be.

He searched the galley and found plastic wrap. Quickly he stretched it out, added the wads of cash from the first bag and then wrapped it, over and over again until the cash was completely covered.

Then he returned it to the bag and did the same to the second bag. At about twenty kilos each, they should sink to the bottom of the ocean.

He didn't want Zoe to have to lie for him, so he left the bags on the table and rejoined Zoe at the helm.

"All clear?" she asked.

"Yeah. I found some cash though." He showed her the two wads he'd taken and handed her a couple of grand. "Can you put this in your bra?"

She nodded and turned her back to him as he put the rest in his backpack. "For in case we need to bribe someone." He glanced around the area. "See anything suspicious?"

"No. I've been scanning the area, but it doesn't look as if they're coming after us." She took a key from her pocket and handed it to him. "I took the boat key."

He grinned. "Great work." He'd wondered why they hadn't given chase.

He shifted next to her and switched on the fish-finding app on the dash. As it booted up, he said, "Why don't you take the other seat? You look tired." He waited until she shifted to the chair next to the captain's before he sat next to her, checking the compass and coordinates. The fish finder had them at eighteen metres depth.

Easily diveable. Good. He could make a decision later.

He put that out of his mind and focused on the woman next to him. Time to put her at ease. "I can't tell you exactly what happened with Ali and Kamran, but I'll tell you what I can. I want you to feel safe with me."

Chapter 12

Zoe's pulse jumped at the earnest way Heath looked at her. Dobby had obviously called him after their conversation. "I'll listen."

He smiled. "I was doing some work in a country near here."

She almost laughed at the vagueness of his statement. Instead she nodded and waited for him to continue.

"Part of that work put me in contact with Ali, who you shot, and Kamran, the other man in the room."

Her stomach rolled. "Did I kill Ali?"

Heath shook his head. "Your shot was non-lethal. It would have hurt a hell of a lot, but he could have survived. I killed him." It wasn't said with relish, rather with grim acceptance. "Both of them did terrible things to good people. I helped stop them. But when they both should have gone to gaol for life, they were merely demoted."

So both men had been higher in the Iranian navy. "Friends in high places."

Heath nodded. "The highest. Neither was happy about being demoted, hence their reaction to seeing me. There's still an arrest warrant out for the role I played."

She could read between the lines. He must have been working undercover.

"I will never hurt you, Zoe. I know words mean nothing, so I want to tell you something about myself that I've only told a few people."

She couldn't look away from the sincerity in his dark eyes. It drew her in, but he shouldn't have to make himself vulnerable for her. "It's not necessary. I appreciate you telling me what you can, and Dobby helped to calm my frightened imagination."

"You were right to question everything that happened. What you witnessed was horrific, and I'd be surprised if you didn't have fears." He paused for a moment. "I'd like to tell you, if you want to listen."

She nodded, unable to find the right words. She did trust him, but she wanted to know more about him.

The boat bumped over a few waves, and there were lots of lights in the distance, ships with their night lights on.

Despite that, it felt as if they were all alone.

"When I was not much older than Mohammad, my family fled Iran. We were of the Bahá'í Faith and were being persecuted. My parents thought they could find a better life for us elsewhere, and so they arranged for us to be smuggled out of the country into Pakistan." Heath stared through the windscreen.

Zoe waited, knowing more was coming and wanting to give him time to put himself together.

"We travelled in the middle of the night on the back of motorcycles. I was squeezed on one with my mum and our guide. My little sister, who was five, was with Dad and another man. About halfway there, in the middle of the desert, we stopped. Mum was tense so I knew something wasn't right."

His hands gripped the steering wheel as if he was reliving the moment. Zoe almost didn't want to know what happened next.

"Men came out of the darkness. They demanded more money, but we had no more to give. They said they would take payment from my mother."

Zoe wanted to be sick, wanted to stop him talking, but his words came faster now.

"Mum was dragged off the bike behind me. My father tried to stop them and he was shot. Killed and left where he fell for the animals to devour." He swallowed hard as his voice broke. "My sister was crying so I sneaked over to her and held her, covering her ears, while my mother screamed for mercy."

Zoe touched his arm, unable to stop the urge to comfort him. He flinched and then relaxed, and she wrapped her arm around his shoulders to soothe him.

"I can still see the leader's face when I close my eyes," he continued. "Black, squinty eyes, his ring finger on his left hand missing, and a crooked nose like the Wicked Witch of the West." He shook his head. "The only time I watched that movie, the nightmares returned for months."

Tears welled in Zoe's eyes and she blinked them back.

"When it was all done, they put us back on the motorbikes and we crossed over the border to Pakistan and into a refugee camp. I thought we would be safe, but there were pockets we learned to avoid. People were at their most vulnerable, particularly women and children. I lost my faith in that camp and vowed I would always protect others, particularly those who couldn't protect themselves."

She swallowed past the lump in her throat. "I'm so sorry, Heath. For everything you and your family have endured."

"They didn't break us," he said. "My mother healed with the help of friends and built us a life in Australia. We don't talk about those times, but I turned to the military, and my sister wants to change the world through human rights and law." He smiled then and turned to Zoe. "She's likely going to run the UN one day."

The love he had for his sister shone from his eyes and made Zoe like him even more. "I'd love to meet her one day."

"She'd like you." He glanced back at the instruments and cleared his throat. "I hope my story helps you understand that I will do nothing to hurt you or take advantage of you."

Her heart ached. "It does." She wanted to smooth the furrows from his brow and ease the tension from his body.

Heath hesitated and then said, "I have a plan to get us into the UAE."

She frowned at the sudden change in topic. "Can't we just pull up on a deserted beach?"

"No. We need proof we entered the country and we can't dock at any harbour without attracting unwanted attention. The boat's covered in blood and bullet holes, and despite us both holding Australian passports, we're on a stolen boat registered to someone involved in drug smuggling."

All really good points. "What's the plan?"

"I'm going to sink the boat."

Zoe laughed out loud, but when he didn't crack a smile, the laughter died. Cautiously she asked, "What do you mean?"

"We'll pose as a couple who have hired this luxury boat for the week. We were heading to Dubai to do some shopping when the engine exploded and the boat sank. We only just got on board the life raft in time." He pointed to the capsule on the back. "I will row us to shore, but with all the boat traffic closer to the mainland, someone might pick us up. We can go through customs, get our passports stamped and tell the authorities we just want to get home. Then we catch the first flight to Australia."

It made sense in theory, but, "How are you going to make the engine explode?"

He tapped his nose and grinned at her. "Trade secret." He glanced out where the lights were getting closer. "But we'll need to act like a couple. Would you feel comfortable with that?"

Her heart softened even more towards him. "Yeah." She was more than happy to fake a relationship with him. This man was definitely someone she wanted to spend time with. The thought surprised her a little, given the circumstances.

Heath smiled at her. "Good. I need to clean up and pack a bag full of things we might have grabbed in a panic before disembarking. Will you be all right up here?"

She really didn't want to be left alone, still half-expecting someone to appear from the darkness to attack again. She swallowed down the fear. "Of course. What can I do to help?"

"Come up with a backstory for us. We probably met in Canberra before you were posted out here and I surprised you by turning up unannounced and whisking you away on this adventure."

She smiled. "And we made it out before everything erupted in Qatar, which is why I can't go back."

"That's right. I won't be long. Steer clear of any vessels. It's going to get pretty busy as we get closer to Dubai, but I'm hoping a lot of the big ships will be at anchor waiting their turn in the port."

Zoe scanned the area as she shifted into the captain's seat. It would take some time before they were close enough to any vessel to worry. "Go. I'll be right here waiting." She smiled at him, hoping to give off a confidence she didn't entirely feel.

"Thanks."

Heath headed down the ladder, and a minute later the light went on in the bedroom. She focused on the dark sea ahead of her, looking for any navigation lights, which would indicate a ship was near.

They were almost safe. By this time tomorrow they'd be on a plane heading for Australia. Would Heath want to see her again after this?

Where would she be? She had no home and she suspected she'd have no job after missing the rendezvous. Her future was unclear and unplanned.

It was almost freeing in a way.

She glanced behind, searching the darkness for movement on the water or navigation lights to show a boat was approaching.

Nothing.

She exhaled. Perhaps the naval vessel didn't have a spare set of keys.

The light in the bedroom flicked off. Heath must have had the quickest shower on record.

Zoe waited for him to reappear, but he didn't. Perhaps he was seeing what else he could salvage. Half of the things in his backpack screamed military training, and her backpack had an embassy laptop in it that thankfully the Iranian navy hadn't seized.

All she had on her were the long-sleeved shirt and pants she'd found in a cupboard and her phone that was on its last battery. Though she had kept the cable ties in her bra just in case.

A lot of evenly spaced lights in the distance

indicated a cargo ship or oil tanker. They must be nearing the coast and were hopefully already into UAE waters.

Heath appeared on deck with his backpack and went over to the life raft at the back. He checked it over, nodded as if satisfied, and then headed up the ladder to Zoe.

He wore all black now, but it was loose linen clothing similar to what Zoe wore. He checked their progress. "We're getting close now. We don't want to be too near in case someone sees what we've done." He glanced behind. "The boat needs time to sink before we're rescued. We should be good here." He put the boat into neutral and turned off the engine. "Come with me."

Zoe followed him to the life raft.

"You jerk this rope to deploy the raft," he said.

Concern filled her. "Where are you going to be?"

He smiled. "Hopefully with you, but just in case…"

She shook her head. "What do you mean? How dangerous is blowing up the engine?"

"There's always a risk, but it will be minimal." He winked at her and said, "I'll be right back."

Zoe stepped after him before catching herself from reaching out. He was trained. He'd probably blown up a million things in training and real life, making use of whatever was at hand.

Still her chest was tight as he disappeared into the cabin. She turned her attention to the capsule in front of her. She really hoped the owners of the boat had regularly serviced their life raft—if life rafts were supposed to be serviced. Zoe heard a splash behind her.

Her breath whooshed from her and she whirled around, only to find Heath on deck heading towards her.

"What was the splash?" she asked.

"Getting rid of some ballast." He waved at her to stay there. "I'll join you in a second." He headed up the ladder to the wheelhouse instead of coming over to her.

She grabbed the rope she was supposed to pull and glanced at the dark water below. Anything could be under there.

Heath started the engine, and the whole boat shuddered as a loud explosion ripped down below. Zoe stumbled, and by the time she'd righted herself, Heath was by her side.

"Pull the rope."

She yanked on it, and the canister rolled down the ramp and over the side. It burst open and an orange life raft inflated. Heath helped her down to the marlin board at the back and pulled the life raft towards them. "Get in."

Heart racing, she did as he asked, awkwardly climbing into the smallish space and moving to the far side to make room for Heath. There were two paddles inside and an emergency light flashed on the outside but barely illuminated the small area. She spotted a light on the inside but couldn't get it to turn on.

"I'll be right back."

Zoe gasped as Heath jogged up the steps and back into the cabin. What the hell was he doing? The boat was sinking.

Though it didn't really look like it was sinking. She couldn't hear any rushing water or see it listing to the side.

What if the explosion hadn't penetrated the hull?

A couple of loud bangs and Zoe held her breath, waiting for Heath to reappear. The raft had floated away from the side of the boat, still attached by the rope, and the boat started to lean.

Definitely sinking now.

"Heath!" She grabbed the rope and pulled the raft back towards the boat, ready to climb on board.

Heath appeared on deck and jogged towards her as if he had all the time in the world. He climbed onto the raft, cut the rope tying them to the boat, and pushed them away.

Zoe sighed in relief and punched his shoulder. "You scared the hell out of me."

"Worried about me?"

"Of course I was worried. I heard bangs. You could have been knocked unconscious."

"The bangs were me widening the hole to make it sink faster." He grabbed one of the oars and started rowing in the direction of the shore. "We want it to sink before someone tries to tow it to shore."

It was impossible to see its progress as five of the six walls of the raft were completely enclosed and it was very dark now they were turned away from the vessel. Zoe tensed, breathing slowly to keep the panic at bay. She wasn't completely enclosed. The entrance was right there. She shifted closer to the small opening, but it unbalanced the boat.

"I've got this," Heath said. "You can take over when I need a break."

She shook her head and gasped for breath.

"Hey, what's wrong? We're safe." Heath ran his hand down her arm. "Shit, is this too enclosed?"

Zoe nodded and instantly he shifted away from the opening, pulling her towards it. "Take some deep breaths."

She inhaled the fresh air, staring up at the dark sky. Not enclosed. Not underground. Safe.

"Do you want to talk about it?"

He'd been vulnerable with her. She could do the same with him. She took another deep breath. "I was about ten," she said. "Dad was working in Coober Pedy, and when he finished, we flew out to meet him and we were going to road trip home."

"Long trip with four kids," Heath commented.

"Yeah, but Mum and Dad knew how to keep us entertained." She remembered the audiobooks, music and travel board games. "We went to the museum and there was a tunnel there to show what it was like for miners underground. I refused to go into it, and my sisters made fun of me incessantly."

"Can't say I blame you. Those opal miners were tough." His calm tone helped to soothe and slow her heart rate further.

"We got back to our accommodation, and still my sisters kept teasing me, saying I was a scaredy-cat." She'd wanted them to stop, to prove she was brave. "People have fossicked for opals on the outskirts of Coober Pedy for decades. There are all these hills and holes left over from that time and my parents told us we weren't to go anywhere without them."

Heath's hand tightened for a second on her arm.

"I figured that to prove how brave I was, I'd

walk into the desert."

"Where were your parents?"

"They were finalising some things at Dad's work." She sighed. "I really wasn't far from the accommodation before I fell into a shaft and the dirt collapsed around me."

Heath swore. "That must have been terrifying."

Her pulse hitched at the memory of the dust and darkness, of being buried alive. "Yeah. There was a small side shaft I hid in, but it took almost a day to find me and get me out. I was fortunate my sisters could pinpoint where I disappeared."

"That's why you've been questioning your instincts," Heath said. "Because one defiance as a child buried you alive."

She coughed out a laugh. "It was pretty traumatic."

He chuckled. "Yeah, but you were a kid. We all do stupid things when we're kids."

"If I hadn't defied Stefan, we wouldn't be sitting in a life raft in the Persian Gulf," she pointed out.

"And those kids wouldn't be on their way home to their parents," he argued. "You've got great instincts; convincing Ali not to take the kids, drugging your guards, shooting Ali. You need to trust yourself as much as I trust you."

Her heart warmed and she shifted back from the entrance so he could continue to row. "You no longer consider me a pain in the arse?"

He chuckled. "Not in the slightest."

She shrugged out of her backpack. "Thank you for everything, Heath."

"It's my pleasure, Zoe."

The oar barely made a splash as he moved them through the water with fast efficiency. The quiet soothed, and the rest of the tension left Zoe's body. She was safe here in this moment.

A few minutes later, Heath turned the raft to look back at the boat and it was already three-quarters submerged.

"Nice work," Zoe said. Impressive really. As they watched, it sank under the inky blackness.

Heath grinned and continued paddling them towards the shore. "So tell me what backstory you came up with for us."

***

Zoe had come up with a backstory that made sense and was easy enough to remember. They'd had a whirlwind romance when she'd gone home to visit family recently, and therefore they didn't know much about each other. It was early days.

Perfect really. Fewer lies to be caught out on if they were questioned at all.

His muscles burned in that extended exercise way, but it was a good burn, productive. He had hoped a fishing vessel might have picked them up by now, or that one of the cargo ships might have spotted them and called out the Dubai sea rescue.

He could see the port clearly, and there wasn't far to go.

He spun the raft around, doing a sweep of the area, and spotted a small fishing vessel heading towards them.

Zoe shifted so she could see better. "Will they pick us up?"

Heath stopped rowing and grabbed his binoculars so he could get a better look. A few men were on deck, but they weren't armed as far as he could see. "Maybe." He checked the multi-tool was in easy reach in his pocket. "Have you still got your tool?"

She nodded and tapped her pocket.

Good. "Can you fit it in your bra?"

She didn't hesitate, reaching into her pocket. He turned his back to give her privacy and said, "Let me speak when they come. We don't know how they're going to react."

Zoe pulled her scarf out of the backpack and covered her hair.

Heath tucked the binoculars into the bag and then waved to the vessel, calling out in Arabic.

"Help. Please help us."

The engines slowed, and one of the men at the bow threw out a rope to them. Heath caught it and tied it to the raft before pulling them in. "Thank you, thank you," he called as they hung a rope ladder from the side.

He turned to Zoe. "Let me go first to assess the situation. Grab on to the ladder after I go up but wait until I tell you to climb." He slipped his backpack on.

"All right."

He grabbed the ladder and pulled himself to his feet and stepped onto the first rung. He waited there for a second for Zoe to shift over to the entrance and then climbed quickly. At the top he was helped aboard by two weather-worn older men. Scanning the deck, he spotted another at the helm and one on the far side fixing a net.

He waved Zoe up and turned to their rescuers. "Thank you for your help."

"What happened?" the man with a fully grey beard asked.

"I don't know. We were on our way to Dubai for a holiday, and there was a loud explosion. We only just had time to get onto the life raft before the boat sank."

The other man studied him. "Where are you from?"

"We came from Qatar today, but we're both from Australia." He helped Zoe onboard and slid an arm around her, holding her close. She leaned into him as if they truly were a couple, and her warmth against him felt right.

"We're heading back to the docks," the old man said. "You can talk to customs there."

Heath nodded. "Thank you so much."

They followed him into the small cabin on the boat, and Heath let Zoe sit first before sitting next to her. The cabin was well worn, smelled like salt and fish, and had nothing in it that raised an alarm.

The man left them there and went back on deck to finish packing up after their day of fishing. It was getting close to ten o'clock at night. If all went well at customs, they could be on a flight home before morning.

"What's next?" Zoe asked, scootching closer so she didn't have to talk loudly.

"Customs," he said. "We've both got our passports, so hopefully it won't take long." He wasn't sure what the officials would want to do about the sunken boat. They might insist on some sort of incident report or insurance claim, but the story was that he'd borrowed it from a friend of a friend who was going to be pissed off it was now at the bottom of the ocean.

He hadn't dared to grab anything extra from

the boat in case it could be traced back to the owners. Instead he took what he thought would be understandable for a day pack of doing touristy things; drink bottle, snacks, binoculars, and cash.

"And then what?"

"Then we book on the next flight out of here."

She shifted closer, and he put his arm around her, giving her comfort. She fit so nicely against him.

"Are we safe now?"

He couldn't lie to her. He wouldn't consider them completely safe until they were on Australian soil. "We're definitely safer."

The Iranian navy might have contacts here and have asked them to be on the lookout.

It wasn't long before the engine tone changed and they were coming into the harbour. Heath scanned the jetties and as the boat pulled into their pen, he spotted two customs officials waiting on the dock.

"Showtime." He pointed to the men. "Let me do the talking."

"Sure."

Heath waited until the boat was tied up and the engine was off before he took Zoe out on the deck. He called a greeting to the officials.

"We need you to come with us," the younger one said.

"Of course." Heath turned to the old fisherman and shook his hand. "Thank you again for saving us."

"Afwan."

They disembarked and followed the officials off the docks into an office at the end.

One step closer to freedom.

Chapter 13

Zoe's Arabic was good after spending so much time in Qatar, but she struggled to keep up with the conversation between Heath and the officials.

They'd been brought into an interview room with a plain grey desk and a few plastic chairs, and Heath had told the officials what had happened. He produced their passports, which were taken away by another official, and had then been questioned incessantly about who he'd hired the boat from.

Perhaps it was a known drug-smuggling boat.

Zoe kept her hands in her lap and her eyes down at the desk in respect as the questioning continued.

"Please, may we go home?" Heath asked after an hour of going back and forth over the details.

"To Qatar?" the official asked.

Heath shook his head. "Zoe's boss called us not long after we left to say they were shutting down the embassy. We'll go back to Australia."

"You're not going to continue your holiday?"

Zoe shuddered and shook her head, and Heath took a moment to squeeze her shoulders. "I think we've had far more adventure than we bargained for. Zoe just wants to see her parents."

Had Dobby told him that? Tears welled in her eyes and she glanced up at him. Her smile felt tremulous, and she sniffed and glanced at the official, and then back down again. But she'd spotted sympathy in his eyes.

Maybe that would help. She just wanted to be on a plane home.

The official who had taken their passports finally returned to the room. He nodded as he handed them to the official interviewing them.

"I'll organise a car to the airport," the man said, handing Heath the passports. He stood and Heath shook his hand vigorously.

"Thank you so much."

Zoe got to her feet, smiled and nodded her thanks at the official and followed him and Heath out of the room.

"Wait here."

The reception area was large, and there were a number of people inside despite the late hour.

A couple of minutes later the official returned. "Your car is ready. It will drop you at the airport.

There are several flights to Australia in the next few hours."

Heath held out his hand. "Thank you for your help."

Outside the building, Heath studied the driver and then slid into the white sedan, holding his hand out for Zoe. He pulled her close.

Warmth rushed into her, which was quickly squashed as he leaned over her and waved goodbye to the official.

All for show.

Of course it was.

He strapped in, greeting the driver and asking him about his day. As the two of them conversed, Heath slid his hand into hers and squeezed it.

She glanced at him, and his warm smile melted her insides.

Maybe it wasn't all for show. Zoe closed her eyes and relaxed on the twenty-minute ride to the airport. Finally they were somewhere safe. All they had to do was get on a plane and fly home.

As the car pulled up to the curb outside departures, a man dressed in a business suit came over and opened the door. Security. "Mr Ghanooni. Ms Yelton. I'm to see you through security." His name badge said his name was Lotfi.

Making sure they left the country.

After they got out of the car, Heath slipped his hand back into hers as if they really were a couple. Zoe smiled and followed the security man into the busy check-in area and over to the Emirates desk. Lotfi spoke to the woman behind the counter. "They're going to Australia."

"Which city?"

"Perth," Heath said. He handed over their passports and the woman booked their tickets.

"It leaves at five," the woman said as she handed them boarding passes.

They had a couple of hours.

Lotfi took their passports and with a smile, he said, "This way."

Worry filled her and Zoe hesitated, glancing at Heath. Keeping their passports spoke of controlling their movements.

She swallowed hard and hurried after them. Heath stopped so suddenly that Zoe bumped into him and tripped. As she righted herself, she noted his whole body was stiff. Concerned, she glanced at his face to find his gaze locked on someone across the building, his expression a picture of fury.

Goosebumps leapt to her skin as she followed his gaze to a maintenance man standing with his trolley next to a water station. The man turned his head and Zoe saw his profile. Crooked nose reminiscent of the Wicked Witch. Her gaze dropped to see his left ring finger was missing.

Shit.

Surely that couldn't be the man from all those years ago.

Heath looked ready to attack. Which wouldn't help either of them.

Quickly she slid her hands around his fist and stepped in front of him. "Heath, look at me."

He didn't move, and she ran her hands down his arms, trying to break through his trance. "Heath, if it's him, you can't do anything here," she murmured. "They'll arrest you." She stood on her tiptoes to block his view. "Please."

He blinked and his breath exploded from him, but the tension remained.

Zoe glanced towards the official who had realised they'd stopped and was waiting for them to catch up. She needed a distraction. She cupped Heath's face, turning it towards her and brushing a kiss onto his lips. He blinked and his gaze shot to hers, surprise in it. "Lotfi is watching us." She grabbed her phone from her pocket and said loudly, "Take a photo with me, honey, to celebrate going home." She pulled him around so they both faced away from the maintenance man, and she zoomed her phone in. Then she held it up, but she couldn't get a good angle on the man. "You have access to facial recognition, right?" she whispered.

Heath shook himself and took the phone. "Let me, darling." He took a photo of the man, but just as he lowered the phone, the battery went dead.

Shit. Had they captured the photo?

"Let me get one with my phone," Heath said.

"Let's go," Lotfi said, walking over and blocking the shot of the suspect.

Heath took the photo and turned. "Sorry about that. I appreciate your patience."

Gone was the angry, frozen man of seconds ago, and in his place was a genuinely grateful guy. Zoe exhaled but slipped her hand in his in case this was just a façade.

The maintenance man swiped his security card at a nearby door and went inside. No way for Heath to confront him, but that was a good thing.

Still if they could identify the man, perhaps he would get some closure. "May I buy a charger?" Zoe asked, pointing to the store they were passing. "My phone is dead and I'd really like to call my parents." She smiled at Lotfi. "It's been an emotional few hours."

Heath squeezed her hand and smiled.

Lotfi looked a little annoyed but nodded and gestured them inside.

"Thank you," Heath said.

"What now?" Zoe asked in a low voice as they wandered away from the man.

***

Heath's mind whirled in disbelief, unable to answer Zoe's question.

It was definitely the same man. Over twenty years older, but still with those harsh eyes, that bump in the middle of his nose that made it crooked and that missing finger.

And there was no denying his visceral reaction to seeing him again.

He'd frozen, completely flashed back to that night in the desert; the darkness, the cold, and the terror.

Until Zoe had brought him back to the now. That's where he needed to stay. "As soon as you've got charge, send the photo to me and Dobby." He scanned the shop for anything that would be useful.

"What about security?" Zoe nodded at their shadow. "Do you think he's going to stay with us until we get onto the plane?"

"Maybe. Though I doubt we're important enough to guard for so long." He grabbed a charger for his phone, some bobby pins and a brush, and some snacks in case they were shut into a room

Whatever happened, he couldn't go after the witch until Zoe was safely on the plane.

He paid and Lotfi led them to a door near the security checkpoint. Heath smiled at the man. "I think we should be good from here. We'll grab something to eat and then wait by the gate for boarding."

The man smiled back. "We have a room you can wait in until the flight."

Damn it. He didn't blame the authorities for making sure they got on the plane, but he wanted to find the witch.

Frustration bubbled in him as Lotfi scanned them through the door, and they walked down a bare, white corridor, passing a few doors on either side until they got to a small room with a table and four chairs in it. Sparse interrogation room.

Lotfi gestured them inside. "There's a power-point you can use to charge your phone." He handed back their passports and boarding passes. "I'll come back when your flight is boarding."

Heath opened his mouth to protest, but the door was shut in his face. He swore under his breath and turned. Zoe had already ripped open her charger packet and put it into the socket.

At least she understood the urgency of the situation.

He called Dobby as Zoe turned her phone on and the device logo appeared on the screen.

"Sitrep," Dobby said.

"Dubai airport. Booked on the five a.m. flight to Perth. Currently sitting in a customs detainment room."

"Why? Have the authorities arrested you?"

"No, they just want to make sure we get on the plane." He kept his voice low and his gaze on the window in the door to make sure they weren't being watched and briefly explained everything that had happened since he'd last called Dobby. "I've found the witch."

Dobby inhaled sharply. "You're sure?"

"Yeah." He glanced at Zoe's phone as she opened her photo app. There he was. Proof Heath wasn't crazy. His phone buzzed with the message she'd sent him and Dobby. "Zoe sent you the photo."

"Send it to Radar too."

Their tech whiz. Quickly he forwarded it.

"Customs won't let you stay behind," Dobby said. "And you can't attack him."

Heath didn't want to acknowledge the truth of his words. It killed him to be this close and not be able to confront the man who'd murdered his father and raped his mother. "Can you ID him?"

"Radar's running it now."

Heath tried the door, but it was locked, not

that they could leave without causing further issues. "We're locked in here."

Dobby swore. "We've identified the guy. You need to get your arse out of there."

Heath went into high alert. "What did you find?" He put the phone on speaker so Zoe could hear and got the plastic card which held bobby pins out of his pocket.

"He's wanted for acts of terrorism, including being suspected for a number of bombings."

Fuck. "He was dressed as maintenance." He had to get Zoe to safety. He started work on the lock.

"Might be taking advantage of the unrest in Qatar and trying to make it spread to other countries. We're calling it in, see if we can get a contact."

At this time of night and with the glacial speed of bureaucracy, it would be too late.

"We need to tell someone." Before he could stop her, Zoe banged on the door and yelled, "Is anyone there?"

"I'll call you back when we get out of here," Heath said to Dobby. He tucked a couple of bobby pins and their hard plastic packaging into his pocket and waited to see if anyone would answer her summons.

If someone came, he'd have to warn them, even if it meant giving away that he wasn't who he'd pretended to be.

Otherwise he'd pick the lock and take them out the way they'd come and leave the airport.

Lotfi came to the window and glanced in, annoyed.

Zoe stepped away from the door and he opened it. "What's wrong?"

Zoe glanced at him.

"There's a known terrorist in the airport dressed as a maintenance worker."

Lotfi's eyes narrowed. "How would you know what a terrorist looks like?"

Heath ignored the question and Zoe held out her phone. "This man."

Lotfi took the phone, glanced at the photo, and then his gaze centred on Heath. "Who are you really?"

His only chance to save hundreds of lives was the truth. "I was hired to get Zoe out of Qatar before the uprising. We ran into a little trouble on the way and ended up here." All truth and enough for the man to know Heath knew what he was talking about.

"I'll be back in a minute." Lotfi left, locking the door behind him and taking Zoe's phone with him.

"Wait!" Zoe called. She turned to Heath. "He can't leave us here when there could be a bomb planted somewhere nearby." She paced the room and on her second pass, he drew her into his arms.

"It's all right. We'll get out of here." He hugged her for a moment until her body relaxed and then let go. "I'm going to unlock the door. Can you put some of these pins under your scarf?" He handed her a couple of bobby pins in case Lotfi caught them and confiscated what he had.

She did as he asked as he set to work on the handle. There was no keyhole on this side, but the hard plastic card might work. There was a little play in the door and he managed to get the card between the door and the wall. He wiggled the card up and down while keeping an eye out for Lotfi returning.

"Grab your charger and get ready," Heath told Zoe.

A shout from down the corridor, followed by two pops. Suppressed gun shots.

Heath swore and grabbed his bag from the table. "Zoe, get over here."

She dashed across the room and he pulled her down next to him, against the wall so they couldn't be seen through the window.

Steps came past but didn't stop. There were no other sounds, no calls of alarm, nothing.

Heath waited a couple of beats more. Next to him Zoe trembled and he rubbed her arm but didn't speak.

He counted out thirty seconds before he stood and peered out. He couldn't see anything out the window but an empty corridor.

He got back to work with the card on the lock and spoke quietly. "When we get out, you follow me. If I say run, you run."

Zoe nodded.

Neither route was safe. Going left would probably take them further into the airport closer to where the witch would plant a bomb, going right would take them closer to an armed shooter.

The door clicked open and he slowly opened it, peering out. The direction the shooter had gone down was empty, but a security guard lay in the other direction.

Heath didn't need to check his pulse to know he was dead. There was far too much blood. He reached for Zoe's hand and she grabbed his.

"We're leaving the airport," Heath said. "Hopefully Lotfi has raised the alarm, otherwise Dobby will have."

Cautiously he jogged down the corridor, pausing at the corner to check it was clear before jogging to the next intersection. They made it without seeing anyone, but he heard shouts of alarm behind them as someone discovered the body.

They finally reached the door out into the

public check-in area. Cautiously he peered through.

It didn't look any different from before. No one was stopped from going through security, and no one was stopped from entering the building.

Maybe the alarm hadn't been raised.

Heath scanned the area, taking in all the families around him, and spotted a maintenance man exiting the building.

He couldn't be sure it was the witch, but he followed with Zoe right behind him.

"There's a—" His shouted warning was cut off as a loud explosion thundered through the area and the whole building shook.

****

Zoe stumbled into Heath as the building shook around them. People screamed, yelling for loved ones, but before she had time to register any damage, Heath was pulling her towards the exit.

She barely had time to get her feet moving in the right direction.

As they burst through the doors, Heath swore and abruptly changed directions. Instead of following the witch, he dragged her across the road in the opposite direction.

Her breath came in pants as she pushed herself after him, unable to form any words.

Behind them another explosion went off, and screams filled the air.

Heath pushed her behind a concrete pillar as debris flew past them. He grunted and pressed his body hard against hers, a human shield.

"Heath."

"Stay still," he said, peering out around the pillar as things stopped flying by.

All Zoe could hear were screams above the ringing in her ears. "What happened?"

"He dropped another bomb in the rubbish bin outside the airport," Heath said. "It's why I changed direction."

How horrific. People would be fleeing the other bomb and run straight into that one.

Her stomach revolted and she gagged.

Heath stepped away, giving her space to breathe and she bent over, sucking air into her lungs, but it was filled with exhaust and dust.

Heath's gaze was in the direction the witch had gone. Zoe glanced towards the airport. People massed at the glass doors, glancing both ways, too scared to exit the building.

"What now?"

"The terminal will close. We're not going anywhere tonight."

Sirens sounded in the distance. People stumbled around, confused.

"Are you all right?" Heath studied her.

She straightened and nodded. "Of course."

"We need to leave." He slipped his hand into hers, but didn't move, his gaze on a small girl crying next to her mother, who had blood streaming down her face.

"We need to help people," Zoe said.

He hesitated as if at war with himself, and then turned, barking orders at taxi drivers who were staring in shock at the destruction. "Clear the way. Get people out of here."

Organising, so cars wouldn't block the way for emergency vehicles.

Already airport staff were running around carrying first aid kits, but there weren't many. Some people were hysterical, and one lady was screaming at her husband to get her out of there while their three young children cried around them. Others helped the injured.

Too many people. They needed to clear them out so that the emergency services could deal with the injured.

Zoe hailed one of the taxis and hurried over to the hysterical woman. "Are you uninjured?"

The woman wailed, but the man nodded.

"Take the taxi into town and find a hotel for the rest of the night," Zoe said. "You can organise new flights in the morning, or drive to Abu Dhabi and get a flight from there."

The husband nodded his thanks and herded

his family into the waiting taxi.

Nearby another couple saw what was happening and hurried over to a taxi.

Zoe moved through the area, speaking to people who seemed frozen in shock, suggesting they leave and return in the morning. Most just needed a nudge to get moving. Those who could, helped others. Those who couldn't or wouldn't, began to clear out.

There were so few medical supplies, but it seemed the worst injured were those who'd been near the rubbish bin when it exploded. A few others had shrapnel wounds, but nothing too serious.

People trickled, then gushed out of the airport. They pushed and shoved in their panic to escape. Zoe hurried away from the doors, but directed people away from the entrance road and injured people. Some listened, others didn't.

Bedlam.

She glanced around for Heath, but couldn't see him amongst the throng. A frisson of concern filled her, and she reached for her phone. No, Lotfi had taken it.

How would she find him in the crowd?

She moved away from the doors and towards the pillar they had sheltered behind.

She reached it just as Heath did. "There you are." He huffed out a breath. "You need to stay close to me."

"Those people needed direction."

He dragged her into his arms and hugged her. "Sorry, you scared me when I couldn't find you."

She hugged him back, the warmth of safety flooding her, and rested her head against his chest. "Do you think there's more danger?"

He shook his head. "I need to keep you in my sights for my own peace of mind. Every time I think we're safe, something else happens."

She glanced up at him. "We'll get through this together."

Their eyes met, and a charge passed between them. It felt like the most natural thing in the world to rise up on her toes and press her mouth against his.

His lips were soft and responsive as he kissed her back, and then deepened the kiss, tightening his hold around her.

Yes. It was right. Passion flowed through her body.

Then a siren wailed near them, and Heath broke the kiss and shoved her against the pillar, his body protecting her again as he glanced around.

Zoe's breath left her, but a moment later he

relaxed his hold.

"Late fire alarm," Heath said, glancing down at her. "Sorry."

She smiled at him. "Don't apologise for your amazing reflexes."

He nodded, suddenly serious. "We need to come up with a new plan."

As much as she'd like to spend the night kissing him, he was right. "Have you checked in with Dobby?"

"Sent him a text."

Ambulances started arriving and the worst injured were seen to. The mass exodus was slowing. Most weren't waiting for taxis, simply hurrying away from the terminal towards the city.

"What do we do now?"

"I think emergency services have got it covered," Heath said.

Zoe nodded, scanning the area. She frowned as she spotted someone next to two men in Dubai Police uniforms. "Is that Lotfi?" She'd thought he'd been shot, but he was scanning the crowd looking fit and healthy.

Heath swore and dragged her behind the pillar out of sight. "It is."

"How?"

"It mustn't have been Lotfi's body on the ground. I assumed, but didn't check."

"Should we tell him we saw the witch put the second bomb in the bin?"

"I'm not sure that's the best idea."

Zoe frowned. "Why?"

"Think about it from his perspective. He gets two Westerners who arrived under suspicious circumstances and are spouting there's a terrorist in the airport. He goes to investigate and when he gets back, he finds a colleague dead, the two people gone, and two bombs have exploded."

Her gut clenched. "We're going to be suspects."

"Yep."

"But we didn't have any guns. We couldn't have shot the worker."

"I'm not sure that matters right now. They'll want to question us again."

"Shouldn't we tell them what we know?"

He sighed. "I want to get you on a plane out of here," he muttered. "I need you to be safe."

Her heart warmed. "The feeling's mutual, but it's the right thing to do."

Heath's phone rang, and he answered.

Whatever the person said had to be bad news because his expression darkened and he scanned the area. "Copy."

He grabbed her hand. "We're getting out of here."

Chapter 14

This mission was cursed from the get-go. Dobby's call confirmed it. They had just been identified as suspects in the bombing of the airport.

Lotfi had to be working with the witch. It was the only thing that made sense, since they'd given him the photo of the bomber and told him who he was.

He must have warned the man, and one of them killed the other security guard.

Which meant they had to avoid him and every person dressed in a uniform.

Airports in the UAE were off the cards for them now. As was a border crossing.

They needed their own transport.

There was a line at the taxi rank with police there to make sure people didn't get violent in their attempt to get away.

Just across from them was a car park full of luxury cars, but it was at a gridlock as people were trying to get out.

Enough people were streaming away from the airport, and they should be able to hide amongst them.

He just wished they'd had a chance to change.

Heath pulled Zoe along with the next group who walked past their position, angling them so the other group was between them and Lotfi.

"What happened?" Zoe asked.

"We're chief suspects," Heath told her, enjoying the feel of her hand in his. He shouldn't have kissed her though. It was unprofessional. She was his mission, he held her safety in his hands.

It didn't matter that she'd initiated it. They were in a situation of high emotions, and he couldn't take advantage of it.

No matter how much he wanted to kiss her again.

He kept monitoring their surroundings and moved quickly through the car park and out into the city. At this time of night the only traffic was to the airport, and aside from emergency vehicles and people leaving, it was quiet.

They had left the crowds behind in the car park and jogged across the road and into the streets beyond.

Zoe was huffing next to him, and he slowed his pace as the streetlights became further apart, and they were able to hide in the darkness.

"What now?" Zoe whispered.

"We need to find a car and drive to the Oman border." Dobby was keeping his ear close to the ground, and Heath knew a guy on the border who owed him a favour. They might be able to charter a flight to Pakistan.

He crossed to a car parked on the side of the road. After a quick sweep of the area, he jimmied the door. When no alarm sounded, he unlocked the passenger side. "Get in."

Zoe hurried around the other side as he hotwired the older model car. He'd left Axle's tool on the boat, knowing it would raise questions he couldn't answer.

In moments they were driving away from the airport. He passed Zoe his phone. "We need to get to Al Ain. It's on the border with Oman."

She plugged in his phone and navigated them away from the airport. Heath kept a close eye on his mirrors to make sure no one was following but gave a quiet exhale.

"Why Al Ain?"

"I know a guy there," Heath said. "We can't use the usual border crossing as you have to pay an exit fee and they'll want to see our passports."

"And they'll detain us."

"Yep."

"Will we have to cross the desert?" Zoe asked, her tone resigned.

He grinned. "Hopefully not."

It took less than ten minutes to get on the highway heading to Al Ain. He knew the way from here. "Call Dobby for me."

She put the phone on speaker, and Dobby picked up immediately. "Where are you?"

"Heading to Al Ain."

"Didn't Hamza go legit?" Dobby asked.

"I'm hoping he'll do me a favour." He had plenty of cash from the boat to sweeten the deal.

"Plan?"

"Hop to Pakistan. Depending on status, flight from there, or drive to India and fly."

"I'll get the usuals to listen to chatter and keep you informed."

"Thanks."

"Dobby, did the kids make it back safely?" Zoe asked. "Are you in Australia?"

Heath should have thought to ask for her.

"Yeah. The embassy staff and team are back in Australia, and Rambo sent out a tugboat to pick up the kids. They're at the port now, waiting for the violence to die down before they take them home."

Zoe exhaled. "Thank you."

"I'll report when we get to Al Ain." Heath hung up. "If it wasn't for you, those kids would still be in that container."

She gave him a wry look. "I'm pretty sure I couldn't have done it without you."

"A joint effort. The Iranian navy wouldn't have given you so much trouble if I hadn't been there."

Zoe muffled a yawn and then asked, "Hop to Pakistan?"

She must be exhausted. They'd been going non-stop for hours. "Charter flight. My contact in Al Ain has a small plane."

Her eyes widened. "To Pakistan?"

"It's only about six hundred kilometres. A few hours."

"But over the ocean."

"He knows his way. Has been doing it for years."

"Smuggler?"

"Previously. Now he legitimately imports goods from Pakistan that Pakistani migrants can't easily get here." He got paid for it, but it was a nice thing to do to help people feel at home.

"Why would he help us?"

"I helped him out of a jam a few years ago."

She chuckled. "Let me guess, you can't give me any details."

He smiled. "No, but let's just say he owes me. Why don't you close your eyes and rest? I know the way from here and I don't know how much opportunity we're going to get to sleep over the next day."

"It's our word against Lotfi's, isn't it?" she asked.

"Yeah, and he's probably erased all footage of the witch by now."

She nodded and settled into her seat. "I'll rest my eyes, but wake me if you need anything."

"Will do, sweetheart."

She smiled and closed her eyes. "Thank you for protecting me, Heath."

The quiet words touched his heart.

"Any time."

***

It took just over an hour to reach Al Ain. The town was quiet and dark at this time of night with only the streetlights lighting the way. Heath wasn't expecting any trouble, but he drove by Hamza's house first as a matter of course. No lights were on, and the gate into the walled compound was closed.

Good.

He drove around the block and parked the car behind the house in an area it wouldn't be noticed.

Zoe woke and glanced outside. "Are we there?"

"Yeah, but I want to go in first, make sure there are no issues." He glanced around the neighbourhood. It was nicer than some, with small compounds and apartment blocks, but not luxurious. Zoe should be safe waiting in the car, but with the way their luck was going, someone would have reported the car stolen and the police would drive past. "I'll go in the back way and check out what's going on, and you can hide nearby."

They were both dressed in dark clothes which made blending into the shadows a little easier.

"Stay a couple of steps behind me," Heath told her.

He moved quickly and lightly over the dirt, staying away from the streetlights and closer to the walls that cordoned off each yard.

When he got closer to Hamza's place, he stopped behind one of the few trees in the street for Zoe to catch up. "Wait here," he said. "I'm going to do some reconnaissance. Stay low against this tree until I come back for you." The street was empty and dark. She should be safe here. "Can I borrow your multi-tool?" His had been confiscated.

She handed it to him. "Be careful," she whispered.

He smiled and moved one house over to Hamza's yard. He grabbed the edge of the wall and pulled himself up to look over.

Darkness.

He climbed over into the garden.

Houses here were built like fortresses to keep out the heat and cold. He moved over to the kitchen window to see if there were any lights on inside.

Heath didn't know which room was Hamza's bedroom, and he didn't want to scare the children.

The sound of a car door slamming caught his attention. It was coming from the front road, not the road where he'd left Zoe.

Quickly he moved down the side of the building as the entrance gate squeaked open.

Shit.

He ducked behind a palm tree as a man strode across the courtyard to the front door.

Inside at a nearby window, a light turned on and then as quickly was turned off.

Possibly Hamza, realising no good visitors came at this time of night.

The man knocked loudly, brazen, uncaring if anyone heard.

Heath frowned. Whoever it was, they weren't expected.

The man pounded on the door again and

inside Heath heard a child's voice, followed by a female hushing them.

Hopefully Dalia was putting her children back to bed.

The hallway light went on and the door opened. Light spilled outside illuminating the man as Hamza said, "Can I help you?"

Crooked nose, dark clothes. Heath clenched his hands. The witch. It wasn't possible. He should be long gone.

Heath took the multi-tool out of his pocket and flicked up the knife, acknowledging the rage coursing through his body.

The witch pushed himself inside and Heath crept closer to look through the window. "I need a flight."

"I'm sorry, I think you have the wrong person," Hamza replied.

"Don't waste my time," the witch growled, pulling out a gun. "My pilot decided to get drunk, a decision he paid for with his life. The next pilot I went to made the fatal mistake of refusing me." The witch paused a moment to let it sink in. "You will take me to Iran."

Shit. The witch wouldn't hesitate to hurt sweet Dalia, and Hamza's children.

Don't argue with him.

"Of course. Let me get my things."

Heath exhaled as Hamza moved towards the

back of the house. The witch followed him.

There was no way the witch would keep Hamza alive after the flight. He was a witness. Did Hamza realise that?

Heath crept to the front door and peered inside. Both men went into the kitchen at the back.

He moved inside and into a receiving room. They would have to come past to get outside, but if Hamza decided to defy the witch, his family would be in danger.

The bedrooms were between the front door and the kitchen.

Heath looked down the corridor and spotted Dalia tiptoeing towards the kitchen. His pulse hitched.

No.

That would end badly.

He moved rapidly down the corridor, his shoes making no sound on the tiled floor, and slapped his hand over her mouth, pulling her towards him before she had a chance to react. She struggled and he murmured, "It's Darius. Hold still."

Her body relaxed and he pulled her into the nearest bedroom. Two beds, and two children sitting upright, but silent. Keeping his voice low, he said, "I know the man with Hamza. He will kill at the slightest provocation. You need to listen to me."

Dalia nodded and Heath removed his hand.

"What are you doing here?"

He shook his head. "Later. You need to get the children out of here. Stay away from the front door. Hide in the garden." He opened the window, thankful it was of a style that would allow them to climb out.

"Nasir," Dalia whispered her son's name and pointed to the left.

"I'll get him." Heath glanced towards the door. Hamza wouldn't take long to get ready.

The girls were already climbing out of the window. Heath opened the door and heard Hamza asking where in Iran the witch wanted to go.

One glance down the corridor revealed that a teenaged boy was almost at the entrance to the kitchen.

Heath swore under his breath and checked Dalia had left with the girls. There was no way of warning Nasir in time, not without making a noise that would alert the witch.

He had to try.

Heath ran towards the boy, just as Nasir stepped into the kitchen. "I'll go."

Heath ducked next to the door out of sight as Nasir moved further into the room.

"Nasir, no," Hamza said, pain in his voice.

"Who do we have here?" the witch asked.

"Go back to bed," Hamza said.

Heath needed eyes on the room to see where everyone was. He had a knife to the witch's gun, and the man would shoot first.

"Can you fly a plane?" The witch sounded curious.

"Yes," Nasir replied. "I've been flying for a year."

"Interesting. I felt like your father was delaying me. You wouldn't do that, would you?"

"No, sir." A tremble in the boy's voice, as if he'd suddenly realised how dangerous the witch was.

"I'm ready," Hamza said, his voice getting closer. "Let's go."

A shot. Nasir's cry. Something large crashing to the floor.

Heath gritted his teeth and stayed where he was.

"Move!" the witch snarled.

Nasir stumbled out of the kitchen, face pale, tears streaming down his face. He didn't notice Heath as he moved down the corridor.

Then the witch stepped out, gun still raised and pointing at the boy.

Heath dove at him, grabbing the hand with the gun and pointing it away as he quickly disarmed the man.

He kept his fury at bay as he hit him twice, knocking him unconscious. Nasir yelled in fright.

Heath followed the witch to the ground, pulling his arms behind his back. "Nasir, get me some rope, or something to tie him up with," Heath said.

The boy stared at him.

"Now!" Heath barked.

Nasir jumped and ran into a nearby room. Heath used the charging cord from his mobile on the witch's hands and then the cord Nasir brought him on the witch's feet.

"Who are you?"

"A friend. Your mother and sisters are outside." Heath dragged the man back into the kitchen so he could keep an eye on him. Hamza lay on the floor, blood pooling out of his shoulder. His eyes flickered.

Still alive.

Heath squatted next to him and applied pressure to the wound. "Get me towels or bandages and call an ambulance."

Nasir squatted next to him. "He's alive?" Hope and tears in his tone.

"Just. He needs help fast."

Nasir blinked and ran across the room to where a phone was charging on the bench. He threw a couple of tea towels at Heath while he called the emergency services.

"Darius?" Hamza croaked.

"Save your breath," Heath said. "You can ask your questions later." There was a lot of blood, but the actual bullet hole was near his shoulder, and hopefully missed anything vital. "You're lucky." Perhaps he'd dived out of the way at the last minute, and the witch was in too much of a hurry to finish him off.

"Ambulance and police are on their way," Nasir reported as he handed Heath a first aid kit.

Heath couldn't be here when the police arrived. There'd be more delays and the witch might have friends in powerful places. "Call your mother inside."

He found a bandage and helped Hamza to a seated position. Nearby the witch stirred.

Quickly Heath cut Hamza's shirt off him and bandaged the wound. Dalia gasped as she brought her daughters into the room.

"He's going to be all right," Heath assured her. He moved over to the witch to ensure he had no other weapons on him and stared down at him.

No sense of satisfaction now he'd finally caught the man. He was numb. He'd stopped the witch from hurting another family, but how many people had he hurt over the decades?

Would he even remember Heath's family in a long line of his horrific actions?

It didn't matter. He needed to get back to Zoe and make sure she was safe.

"You're making a mistake," the witch said.

Heath glanced at him, his expression hard. "My only mistake was not tracking you down sooner. It's time you paid for all those you've killed and raped."

The man's eyes widened, but he said nothing else.

Heath checked the man's restraints. "This man blew up the airport," he told Dalia. "Make sure you tell the police."

"What are you doing here?" Dalia asked.

He chuckled. "Same thing as this guy. I need a flight out of the country. They were trying to pin the bombings on me."

"He's lying," the witch said. "He did bomb the airport."

Dalia kicked him. "We know this man. He would never do such a thing."

Heath drew the family away from the witch and lowered his voice. "The authorities will want to take me in for questioning, but I have someone I need to protect, someone who needs to get home."

"I will take you wherever you want to go," Hamza said.

Heath shook his head. "You need to have your wound seen to," he said. "I need to get across the border."

Hamza beamed at him. "Nasir will fly you, my friend."

***

Heath disappeared over the wall like it was a waist-high fence, not a bigger than he was brick structure, and for the first time in hours Zoe was alone.

In the dark.

In a completely foreign country, in a town she knew nothing about.

If something happened to Heath…

She shoved away her worry for herself and for him. Heath was amazing at his job. He would be fine.

Still she strained to hear any sounds of what was going on, but the night was still. She shifted out of her crouch and sat, hugging her knees to her chest and her back close as she could to the shrubby tree. At least it gave her cover if someone came along.

Zoe scanned what she could see of the street, but there was no movement.

What if Heath's contact wasn't a friend, and double-crossed Heath?

She slapped down her panic and yawned,

placing her hand over her mouth to muffle the noise. The brief nap she'd had in the car only made her yearn for a bed even more.

How long had Heath been gone? It felt like an eternity. Heath might be outnumbered. He might not be able to get free.

How long should she wait before she tried to rescue him?

A faint bang in the night's air, which Zoe would have missed if she hadn't been listening so carefully. She stiffened, leaning forward to hear more, and kept her gaze on the wall Heath had gone over.

What was going on?

She looked around in case Heath was returning from another direction, but the street was still empty.

Not long after she heard the faint sound of sirens in the distance, but they were coming closer.

Had Heath been caught?

Or worse, injured?

She wasn't familiar with the sirens they used for emergency services here, and it almost sounded like there were two, intermingled.

Where was Heath?

Worry intensified, prickling her skin, and she got to her feet as a figure appeared at the top of the wall. She shrank back against the tree.

Definitely not Heath. This figure was scrambling as if they'd never climbed a wall before. They dangled from the top before dropping the short distance to the ground with a grunt.

Too slim to be Heath and the way the person moved made her think they were young.

Another figure appeared, this one almost springing over the wall.

She let out a sigh of relief.

Heath.

He clapped the first figure on the back and then jogged over to the tree. Zoe stepped out and hugged him. "Are you OK? How did it go? What are the sirens for?"

He chuckled. "Yes, fine, the reason we need to get moving." He took her hand and moved them towards the car. "This is Nasir. He's going to fly us out of here."

She glanced at the other figure but couldn't make out his features. It wasn't until they got into the car, and the light switched on, that she saw Nasir was a teenager.

He was going to fly them? Was he old enough to even have a pilot's licence?

Nasir got into the back seat, and Heath drove away from the house and the incoming sirens.

"Will my dad really be all right?" Nasir asked, his concern clear.

"Yeah. The bleeding stopped when I applied pressure."

"What happened?" Zoe asked in Arabic.

"The witch turned up looking for a flight."

She gasped.

"Nasir's father was shot, but he's all right. The witch is tied up."

"He was shot because of me," Nasir said.

Heath shook his head. "The man would have killed your father when they arrived in Iran."

Nasir glanced at him. "But why?"

Zoe's heart went out to him. He was losing his innocence as well.

"Because he doesn't like to leave witnesses," Heath told him. "Why did you go in there?"

"I wanted to help." The words were slightly defiant.

Zoe was missing part of the story, but she'd ask Heath about it later. Right now she wanted to keep Nasir on their side. "How long have you been flying?"

"Dad started training me not long after we met Darius. He wanted to turn the business into a legitimate family business, and I love to fly." He shifted in his seat and pointed. "Turn down there."

Heath followed his directions as they turned into a street near the airport. "Are people going to question why you're flying out at this time of night? I don't want to get you into trouble."

"We've got a flight today," Nasir answered. "I'll just tell them I want to arrive early so I can do some shopping for the family." He pointed to a gate. "Park there."

It would be pretty early for shopping, but Zoe had no idea where they would be landing. Perhaps it was somewhere with early morning markets.

Heath switched the internal lights off, and they got out. Nasir took them through a locked gate and over to a very small plane. Zoe's pulse hitched, and she pressed her lips together to stop herself from questioning it. Heath knew what he was doing.

"There's only one spare seat, so someone is going to need to sit in the back," Nasir said.

"I will. Zoe can be in the front."

Nasir nodded. "Both of you get in the back for now. I need to get the plane ready and file the paperwork. I'll be about half an hour."

Zoe climbed into the back of the small plane. The two doors opened outwards and left a large space for freight. Heath joined her and Nasir shut the door again, and then went around the plane, untying it, removing chocks and running through all sorts of manual checks she didn't understand. At least he seemed to know what he was doing.

She turned her attention to Heath. "Why do we need to fly out if the witch has been caught?"

"The officials could delay us for weeks while they investigate," Heath said. "We don't know what contacts the witch has here. He may get away with it, though the team is pulling on all their contacts to send the government the information we have on the witch. At a minimum, he should see some gaol time for shooting Hamza."

"So we need to keep moving in case they want to arrest us?"

Heath nodded. "We're heading to Pakistan from here. I've got contacts there who will leave a car at the airport for us."

"Can this plane actually fly that far?"

Heath nodded. "It's a twin engine, so it doesn't have to hug the coastline and Nasir will be able to fill up with fuel because there's not much weight going out. He'll refuel in Pakistan."

Zoe didn't know anything about flying. She scootched closer to Heath, needing to be nearer to him. He slipped his arm around her shoulders.

"How are you holding up?"

She shook her head. "This is all going to seem like a crazy dream when we get home."

"I hope not all of it is bad."

"Not all of it." Zoe smiled as she glanced at

him. "I'm glad I met you."

"Likewise. You're incredible, Zoe. Most people would have fallen apart by now."

Zoe chuckled. "I'm not going to lie, I'll probably sleep for a week when we finally get somewhere safe."

He nodded. "See if you can sleep on the journey to Pakistan. I need to check flights home from there, but we'll probably have to drive to Karachi to get an international flight."

"How long will that take?"

"Eight or nine hours."

Her whole body slumped. It would be another day before she could truly stop looking over her shoulder or waiting for someone to stop and arrest them. "Are you going to be OK to drive? You haven't slept at all."

"I'll get a couple of hours now as well. That's all I need."

She shook her head. "You're the incredible one. I don't know how you do it."

"Practice and training." He kissed the side of her head. "You'll be safe soon."

She snuggled closer. The casual affection from him seemed normal, almost as if they'd been a couple for years rather than strangers who'd just met.

She didn't question it.

She felt safe now.

Chapter 15

It was still dark when the little plane landed at a tiny airstrip in Pakistan. Nasir provided their passports with a stamp of arrival—remnants from the days when his father was a less than legitimate businessman—and there was a car waiting for them just as Dobby had promised.

As the plane taxied to a stop, Heath scanned the surrounding area for any sign someone was waiting to arrest them.

All was still.

Nasir pulled the plane to a stop near the car park and turned off the engine. Silence filled the cabin.

"Thank you, Nasir," Zoe said as she unstrapped.

"You're welcome, Zoe," the boy replied.

Heath let the boy open the doors and climbed out before hugging him. "I really appreciate this, Nasir." He pushed a wad of cash into the boy's hands. It would be enough to cover the fuel and extra for his time.

"No, no. You saved my family," Nasir said, pushing the money away. "You owe us nothing."

"I insist. You saved Zoe and me tonight, and we're both grateful." He patted him on the shoulder. "Take care."

Though he would have liked to stay to help Nasir load his freight, he didn't want to attract unwanted attention.

Heath took Zoe's hand in his and they strode over to where the car was waiting. It was a white late-model sedan, which wouldn't win any races, but would blend in nicely and get them to where they needed to go. The keys were above the sun visor, and the engine started with a purr. He opened his maps app and navigated to Gwadar, plugging the phone into the USB port in the car.

"So we've got an eight-hour road trip ahead of us?" Zoe asked, the fatigue clear in her voice.

"Nope, just an hour and a half." He'd spent the first part of their flight figuring out their options. "There's a flight from Gwadar to Karachi at nine. We should make it with plenty of time and be in Karachi by eleven." He glanced around the area. It didn't look as if any officials were going to stop them.

"Thank goodness. How are we getting to Australia?"

"There's a flight to Bangkok at eleven p.m., and then a connecting one to Perth. We should be home by tomorrow afternoon."

Her sigh was long and heartfelt. He squeezed her leg. "Almost there."

It didn't take long to get onto the motorway and in almost no time they had arrived in Gwadar. Zoe was breathing heavily, having fallen asleep almost immediately after they'd hit the road. She really was exhausted.

Fatigue settled over him like a well-worn cloak, familiar and comfortable.

He parked at the far side of the car park where there were a few cars. Zoe woke up and looked around in a daze.

"We're at the airport," Heath told her.

"Already? Did I fall asleep?"

"Yeah." They were a little early for their flight, so hopefully that would give them time to find a change of clothes and a shower. The airport here was brand new, however he couldn't find much about its facilities online.

Zoe brushed her hair back and adjusted her scarf. "Do we just leave the car here?"

"Yeah. I'll let Dobby know where we left it and he'll contact the guy to pick it up."

It was lighter now, and people were arriving for early morning flights. It felt like days ago that they'd showered on the boat, instead of only last night.

"Come on. Let's get some food."

They walked into the brand-new modern building to find a lot of empty shops, but the check-in was modern.

"Hopefully there are more facilities past security," Heath said. He'd bought them tickets online and since they had no checked baggage, they went straight to the security line. The officers there looked bored. Thankfully because it was an internal flight, there was no need for a passport check. Still, he traced their exit route should something go wrong. He slipped his hand into Zoe's and she glanced at him, brief concern on her face.

The security guard yawned and waved them through, and the tension released from Heath's shoulders.

He nodded his thanks and continued into the restricted area of the airport. Here there was one restaurant open this early. They joined the line and bought some paratha and chai, and Heath chose a table in the corner where he could see people coming and going.

Zoe sighed as she sat. "How long did you say we had in Karachi?"

"About twelve hours, which will give us both time to rest."

The hopeful look in her eyes made him add,

"I booked us a room at the airport hotel. We should be safe there."

Tears welled, and she brushed them away. "Thank you. Sorry. I'm overly tired."

He squeezed her hand. "You have every right to be emotional. Now, get some food into you and then we'll go find our gate."

Heath ate quickly, a habit he'd learned when on a mission. If he didn't eat fast, he might not get to eat.

Zoe, on the other hand, savoured every bite as if she'd never tasted anything so good. When had they last eaten?

Maybe at the souq in Doha.

No wonder she was starving.

He'd forgotten about the snacks he'd bought at Dubai airport when they'd purchased the chargers.

He kept half of his attention on the people walking past or dining nearby. No one looked twice at them. With Zoe's head wrapped in the scarf and her facing away from people, no one noticed she was of European descent, and Heath blended right in.

He'd spent a long time in Pakistan as a child in the migrant camps. The food and the smell of chai took him back there. He'd lost his innocence and become a protector there, sticking up for those who were being bullied or teased. He'd returned home in the evenings with a bloody nose, or extra bruises, but his mother only asked him to be careful.

She was still recovering from her own trauma.

Pakistan was a place of in-between, where they were safer than they had been, but not as safe as they could be.

Kind of like now.

A few officials walked past, and various flight attendants and pilots strode to or away from their planes. The departures board showed their gate was boarding as Zoe finished her meal.

She leaned back, satisfied. "That was the best food I've ever had."

He smiled. "Sorry, I should have fed you more."

She shook her head. "You were busy keeping us safe." She glanced around. "I could use a bathroom now."

"There's one over there." He nodded. The thought of being separated from her didn't sit well with him, but he could use the facilities as well. As they walked over he said, "When you're done, if I'm not out here, wait for me right here." He pointed to a chair. "I don't want to freak out and worry that something's happened to you."

She looked around with concern. "Do you think something will?"

"No, but I didn't expect a lot of what happened on this mission." He smiled to show he didn't mind.

"All right. And if something happens to you?"

He handed over her ticket. "You get on the plane to Karachi."

She stared at him, incredulity on her face. "I'm not leaving you behind after everything you've done." She refused to take the ticket. "So make sure nothing happens to you." Her expression was pure defiance as she strode into the female toilets.

Heath stared after her, a smile on his lips and a strange discomfort on his heart. Zoe was everything he could want in a woman; smart, courageous, loyal, and beautiful.

For the first time, he wasn't looking forward to reaching Australia.

It would put an end to their association, and he wasn't certain she would want to see him again, despite the few kisses they'd shared. He represented the period when Zoe had seen the truth of the world, and it might not be something she wanted to remember.

But he wouldn't let her go without at least trying.

****

Zoe felt as if she had finally returned to some

semblance of normal as she stepped off the plane in Karachi. The airport was bustling, no one questioned them being there or even looked twice at them.

"Let's get something else to wear," Heath said as he pulled her into a shop which sold Western clothing.

Fatigue made her brain a little foggy as she stared at the clothes, trying to figure out what she needed.

Heath turned her towards him. "Get something to sleep in now, and something comfortable for the rest of the flight home."

Shopping was a normal activity, but it all felt a little surreal after everything they'd been through.

Still she nodded and grabbed a T-shirt and loose shorts for sleeping in, and then a tracksuit for the flight home. She spotted some underwear as well but glanced at Heath. "Can I use my credit card here?"

He shook his head. "Better not. I've got plenty of cash, so buy whatever you need."

She added the underwear, socks, and a pair of shoes to her collection. She wanted to get out of everything she was wearing and leave all of it behind.

Shedding her skin of the memories they contained.

Heath paid and then took her into a nearby shop to get some toothbrushes and other toiletries before taking her hand. "The hotel is this way."

Her feet felt like there were giant weights on them as she trudged after Heath towards a short line for a bus shuttle service. She shuffled up the steps and took her seat, and only a few minutes later they were disembarking, and checking in to a very nice-looking hotel.

Heath spoke Urdu to the check-in person and Zoe stared into space, the exhaustion finally catching up with her.

All she wanted was a shower and a bed.

She blinked when Heath took her hand and led her to a nearby elevator bank where he navigated them to the right floor and room.

Thank goodness he was still functioning efficiently. Zoe wasn't sure she'd be able to get her phone number right if someone questioned her.

Inside was a nicer than average hotel room with a large king-sized bed. Zoe just blinked as Heath cursed. "I asked for a twin room. Let me call them."

Zoe stared longingly at the bed. Right now she didn't care, all she wanted was sleep.

Heath was arguing with the reception, but it wasn't until he hung up that she understood why.

"They only have this room available."

It took a second for the implication to sink in. There was only one bed. Zoe forced herself to smile at him. "Heath, that bed could fit four people and no one would know the others were in there. We can share."

"I can sleep on the floor."

She shook her head, a little irritation seeping past her fatigue. "Don't be ridiculous. You need to rest as well."

He hesitated, his concern clear in the intensity on his face. "Are you sure?"

"Yes. I'm going to be comatose the second my head hits the pillow." She waved towards the bathroom. "Can I have a shower?"

"Of course."

She took her shopping into the room with her and closed the door before turning on the shower. She glanced at the lock but didn't bother with it. If something occurred, Heath would need to get to her quickly, and she trusted him.

She placed her new clothes on the bench and stepped under the shower, the warm spray running over her.

Pure bliss.

A moment of serenity in an otherwise horrible day.

She turned her head to the spray and closed her eyes. They still weren't in the clear. They had to get through security again when they boarded the flight to Bangkok, and someone might notice a problem with their passport stamps, or they may have been flagged in relation to the Dubai bombing.

She wouldn't truly relax until they were in the air again.

Though it was tempting to soak in the shower, the bed called her more. She got out, dressed in her sleeping clothes, and left the room.

Heath glanced up and smiled. "Feeling better?"

She nodded. "Slightly more human than before." She glanced at the bed. "Do you have a preferred side?"

"Let me sleep closer to the door."

Of course. Always the protector.

"I've set an alarm. I'll have a quick shower and then join you."

Zoe nodded as she climbed under the covers.

Her head hit the pillow, and there was nothing else.

Chapter 16

A loud, insistent beeping shocked Zoe out of a deep sleep. She jolted and found herself being spooned with a warm arm wrapped around her.

Panic filled her for a second as she tried to place where she was and who she was with. The hotel room could be anywhere.

"Shit, sorry." Heath's warm voice identified the arm as he quickly withdrew it and sat up, switching the light on.

Zoe's heart rate slowed as she took a moment to calm herself before turning to face him. "It's fine." Actually it would have been more than fine if she'd realised whose arms she was wrapped in when she woke. She pushed her hair out of her face and smiled at him to show she wasn't bothered. "Did you sleep well?"

He nodded and grinned. "I don't need to ask about you, because you were dead to the world by the time I came out of the shower."

Her cheeks flushed. "It was a long day."

Their gaze lingered and Zoe was mindful of

just how much of a mess she must look right now.

Heath on the other hand, was already clear-eyed and alert.

What would it take to distract him?

Her eyes darted to his lips.

Heath cleared his throat, already climbing out of the bed. "We should get moving," he said. "I don't know how long the lines at security are going to be and we don't want to miss our flight."

That threat was enough to dissolve all her thoughts of how she could distract him.

She wanted to go home. Zoe threw back the covers. "Do I have time for a quick shower to freshen up?" Her eyes felt heavy still, and her muscles were tight, probably because she hadn't moved in several hours.

"Yeah, but don't take too long." He handed her the bag with her travelling clothes.

"Thanks." As she walked to the bathroom, she noticed the exit door had a coat hanger hanging from it. She frowned, and it took her a second to realise it would make noise when someone entered the room.

Early warning system.

Heath was still on active duty. Still thinking about safety while she had been too tired to even think.

Her respect and admiration for him grew.

Now they weren't fleeing for their lives she had time to examine how she felt about Heath.

She wanted to get to know him, wanted to find out what else made him tick. But would he want to see her again after they got home, or was she just a mission—and a pain in the arse —to him?

Pushing her concerns aside, she finished her shower and brushed her teeth, walking back into the hotel room in record time. "Your turn."

She used the mirror in the main room to brush her hair and then put the scarf in place.

She stared at her reflection, noting a faint bruise from where Kamran had backhanded her. She touched it lightly and winced.

It could have been so much worse. Ali or Kamran could have ordered her to be punished as well.

She'd been lucky.

The expression in her eyes grew darker as she ran through all the options. She might still look the same, but something had definitely shifted inside her. The world felt different now. She couldn't go back to her cosy life while knowing that somewhere, someone was probably facing the most horrific day of their life right now.

How was she supposed to reconcile that?

The door opened and Heath walked out, drying his hair with a towel, dressed casually in branded tracksuit pants and a jumper. Casual, yet extremely sexy.

She pushed aside her dark thoughts to focus on Heath. Right now she would enjoy what time she had left with him. "Feeling better?"

"Yeah." He handed Zoe her backpack, and she put her sleeping clothes inside. By the time she turned around to check what else needed to be packed, Heath was by the door with his backpack over his shoulder and one of the shopping bags full of their old clothes inside. "Ready to go?"

Part of her was more than ready to get home, but there was also a part that wanted to stay here, where it was safe, where she didn't have to worry that something else was going to go wrong.

What if they hadn't been cleared of involvement in the Dubai airport bombing? What if there was an international warrant out for their arrest and the moment they went through customs they were arrested again?

Heath didn't look worried. He waited patiently by the door, but perhaps he saw the concern in her eyes because he said, "It's all right. We'll be home soon."

"What about customs?"

"Dobby hasn't picked up any international chatter," Heath said. "There're no warrants for our arrest."

His assurance calmed her anxiety, and she followed him out of the room.

It was dark when they exited the hotel and boarded the shuttle back to the airport. "What time's our flight?" she asked as they walked into the bustling terminal.

Heath placed the bag with their old clothes in a nearby bin. "We've still got a couple of hours."

She frowned. "How long did we sleep for?"

"About eight hours."

She hadn't realised. Her stomach rumbled.

Heath chuckled and passed her a protein bar from his backpack. "We'll get something more substantial as soon as we're through security."

She scanned the other passengers streaming into the airport, partially expecting the witch to turn up here, even though he was back in the UAE. Her shoulders were tense as she walked past another rubbish bin.

Would she ever feel safe in a crowded place again?

There was a part of her that was more aware now and possibly always would be.

Finally it was their turn at the customs desk. Zoe held her breath as Heath handed over their passports. The man stamped them without really looking at them and then they were through to the gate area. Zoe breathed a sigh of relief. Almost out of here.

"What do you want to eat?" Heath asked.

There were a few restaurants available. Something plain that reminded her of home. "How about a burger?" And chips. Comfort food.

"Sounds good."

The service was fast and it wasn't long before they were seated with their food, Heath sat facing the entrance again so he could see the comings and goings.

"Is it second nature?" Zoe asked.

He frowned. "What?"

"You position yourself so you can see everyone coming. You booby-trapped the hotel door too."

He smiled and nodded. "You need to see threats when they're coming. Even when I'm not on a mission, I tend to be aware of my surroundings."

She had to remember this was a mission for him, instead of enjoying being in bed with him and thinking about wanting to see him again.

No wonder he'd leapt out of the bed when they'd awoken. And she'd thrown herself at him at the airport in Dubai, kissing him.

Talk about sexual misconduct. Her face heated. Totally inappropriate thing to do to a man who was doing his job. She'd put him in a difficult position, and now he was probably dying to get her out of his hands.

Maybe she had some kind of hero worship going on, and all the heightened emotions were getting to her.

Damn, she didn't want it to be. She really liked him.

She had to apologise. But this was going to be awkward.

She tilted her head and studied him for a minute, trying to find the right words.

"What? Do I have something on my face?" Heath wiped at his beard.

She shook her head. "No, I'm trying to figure out how to ask you something."

"Go ahead."

"It might make things awkward or weird." She shifted in her seat, suddenly wishing she hadn't brought it up.

He reached over and squeezed her hand. "It's OK, Zoe. You can ask me anything." His eyes met hers, and there was open honesty in them.

She braced herself. "Should I not have kissed you? I mean, the first time I was trying to distract you from the witch, but the second time…" She squirmed. "That was because I wanted to. Was that inappropriate work conduct?" Another thought occurred to her. "Or did you just kiss me back so it wouldn't be awkward?" Oh, that was particularly mortifying.

Heath's lips quirked, but he didn't laugh at her spiralling. He put down his burger and took both of her hands in his. "Zoe, it's OK." He squeezed them. "I'm glad you kissed me, and I wanted to kiss you." His smile was warm before he turned serious. "My major would have a fit if he found out about it, but I'm not planning to tell him. The truth is, I want to get to know you better and was trying to figure out how long I needed to wait after we get back to Australia before it would be appropriate to ask you out."

Her heart sang, but she frowned. "Why wait?"

"I'm in a position of power over you, Zoe. I'm responsible for your safety. I don't want you to feel as if you owe me anything. I won't take advantage of this situation."

Her mouth gaped as she realised what he was saying. "I didn't consider that." But she should have after what he'd been through. Her cheeks heated, and she glanced down at the table and then back at him. "But just for your reference, I'm fairly sure I'll be free all this week for a date."

He grinned at her then, the seriousness leaving his gaze. "Good to know. I'll call you as soon as the debrief is over."

Anticipation stirred, and she couldn't wait to get back to Australia. "How long's that likely to take?"

"No more than a day." He pinched one of her chips. "What kind of dates do you like to go on?"

It had been so long since she'd been on one, she didn't know. "To be honest, I want time to get to know you," she said. "Somewhere we can talk, and eat…" She glanced at the surrounding people, feeling a little exposed. "And be away from crowds."

"I can manage that."

She grinned as she ate another couple of chips, but when she glanced at the burger, her stomach suddenly rolled.

The smell was too… meaty for her. Kamran's face flashed into her mind and she pushed the food away, her appetite gone.

"Are you OK?" Heath asked.

She sipped the soft drink that had come with the meal, not wanting to spoil the mood. "Fine. You can have my burger."

Heath's expression grew sympathetic. "I should have thought of it. The first time for me, I couldn't eat meat for a month." He quickly transferred the burger onto his plate. "There will be food on the plane if you want to wait, or I can buy you something else."

She shifted back in her seat, feeling a little better now the burger wasn't directly in front of her. Was this going to be her life now? Moments that flashed her back to the horror she'd witnessed.

"It will get easier," Heath assured her. "What's the process with the embassy shut down?" he continued. "Will you be working in Canberra?"

Zoe shrugged, bringing her attention back to him, and giving him a small smile to show her appreciation at him changing the subject. "I don't know. It all happened so fast, there was no discussion of what would happen when we got home." She sighed. "I might not have a job at all. Stefan was pretty angry, and I disobeyed a direct order. It's cause for immediate dismissal."

Heath tilted his head at her. "You don't sound upset about it."

"After everything that's happened… the work I was doing doesn't seem very important."

He nodded. "You should see a therapist when you get home. It's important to talk about what happened. Your worldview has shifted, and it will take time to make sense of it."

"How many people do you rescue?" Zoe asked. "How much atrocity do you see?"

He didn't shy away from the question. "A lot, but it's not always this violent. Sometimes we just gather intel."

"Of horrible things or people?"

He nodded. "It helps to know we're doing our

bit to stop it."

Maybe that was what was missing. Maybe if she felt as if she was helping, she wouldn't feel so helpless inside. "What type of law is your sister studying?"

"Human rights. She's talking about volunteering at some of the refugee camps in Turkey or Pakistan."

That took guts. Did Zoe want to be surrounded by danger in order to help people? She wasn't certain. "Do you think she'd be willing to talk to me after we get home?"

"Of course. Leila's always after the next convert." He smiled.

She returned his smile as some of the uncertainty faded, having the next step of a plan in place.

"How long before your next mission?" Zoe asked.

He shrugged. "I never know. It could be weeks, or it could be days. The call for the Doha extraction wasn't expected. Everything escalated pretty fast."

It sure had. She hadn't quite understood the danger when Stefan had spoken of packing up the embassy.

Heath sipped his drink. "There are a few refugee and migrant centres in Perth that help people settle into Australia. They might be a good place for you to start." He smiled. "I still remember the woman who welcomed us to Australia with a sponge cake and a jar of Vegemite." He chuckled.

"An interesting combination."

"I know. Luckily she explained how much Vegemite to use on toast. She introduced us to a bunch of people, helped Mum find a community, and they're still good friends to this day."

That sounded nice. It would be hard to negotiate a new country with an unfamiliar language and customs, particularly when you were grieving the loss of your husband and having to leave your home behind, not to mention any violence that had occurred.

Heath's mother must be an incredible woman.

"Maybe I could talk to her as well."

"Sure. I'll introduce you when you're ready."

It might take time for her to be ready. Zoe was looking forward to seeing her own parents again. It had been a couple of years since she'd seen them. And depending on what happened with her job, they or one of her sisters would have somewhere she could stay. She'd been living in Canberra before she got posted to Doha, so it would be nice to be back home for a while. Nothing beat the relaxed vibe and beautiful beaches of the west coast.

She glanced at Heath. Perhaps she could make it home for the foreseeable future. "How long have you been in special forces?"

He smiled at her. "A while. Though Dobby is about to retire and put together a private security firm."

"Is that code for becoming a mercenary?"

He shook his head, chuckling. "No. It will be more bodyguard work and helping with civilian issues rather than national issues."

"I wouldn't have thought there'd be a lot of need."

"You'd be surprised."

Maybe she would be. She really didn't know what the underbelly of Australia looked like. "Is any of your team joining him?"

"One of my mates has just been medically discharged. He'll join Dobby." Heath ran a hand over his hair. "I'm starting to think I might too."

"Why?"

"Seeing the witch again... the visceral reaction I had, knowing he's probably put hundreds, if not thousands, of people through similar things to what I went through... I can't ignore it."

She reached out and squeezed his hand. "I understand. He deserves to pay for his atrocities, but he's been arrested now."

"We don't know he'll be punished." He turned his hand over and squeezed hers back. "And there are plenty of others out there like him, preying on the vulnerable and desperate." He let go of her hand and ate a chip.

Heath wasn't the type to ignore a problem after he recognised it. She respected him for it. "Do you think we would have spoken much if we'd made it onto the plane on time?"

"Probably not. You would have sat with your people and I would have debriefed with the team."

"Then I'm glad I was late."

"Me too."

They shared a look and the moment pulsed between them. He glanced over her shoulder. "You should finish your food."

And just like that, the relaxed conversation was gone. "What's wrong?" She resisted looking behind her in case she gave something away, but her shoulders tensed.

"Nothing. Sorry to startle you. Gate's open and boarding has started."

She ate a few more chips and then pushed her plate away. "Let's go catch a plane."

Chapter 17

Nothing went wrong before they boarded the plane. No bombs exploded, no delays on their flight, no sudden arrest for a crime they didn't commit.

For that Heath was extremely grateful.

They settled into their seats on the Thai-run airways and even that felt like they'd crossed a border, moving closer to home.

Next to him in the window seat, Zoe read the safety card and then the magazine which came in the pocket.

Heath kept his eyes trained on the door and who was boarding. No officials, no huddled discussions by the flight attendants, no cause for alarm.

When the door finally closed and the plane taxied to the runway, he relaxed a little. Then the plane rumbled down the tarmac, and finally wheels lifted from the ground, and he exhaled. On their way home.

He used the plane Wi-Fi to message Dobby

and finally turned to Zoe. She was dabbing at tears in her eyes. Alarmed, he glanced at her TV screen, but it was blank. "What's wrong?"

She sniffed. "We're going home."

She'd been as uptight as him.

Of course she had. He should have thought of it. Every time they thought they were safe, something else happened. "Yes, we are. In just over twelve hours, we'll be back in Australia."

"Thank you, Heath. Thank you for getting me out of there. Thank you for helping me rescue the children. Thank you for protecting me."

"It was my pleasure."

She gave him a slightly incredulous side-eye, and he chuckled. "Well, not all the shooting, and danger, and running, but helping those children and getting to know you has been one of the best experiences of my life."

Zoe slipped her hand into his. "Same."

His heart sang. He loved how open she was. He hadn't been expecting the upfront conversation they'd had about how they felt about each other. It was a relief, because waking up next to Zoe had been a beautiful torture. Though she'd seemed receptive, he had to keep reminding himself that Zoe was vulnerable and he didn't want to prey on her vulnerability.

In a few more hours, she would no longer be

his mission, and he could act on their attraction to each other.

The attendants started to bring around drinks and food, and he relaxed into his seat the best he could.

He was ready for home.

Just over twelve hours later, after a brief stop in Bangkok where they only had time to get from one gate to the next, the plane touched down in Perth. As the pilot announced the time and temperature, Heath wanted to cheer, but Zoe burst into tears.

Heath put his arm around her shoulders and pulled her close. "It's all right. You're safe now."

She nodded into his chest but didn't say anything.

The poor woman was still overwrought. She'd slept again on the leg to Bangkok and then watched movies on the way to Perth, but she still had to be mentally and physically exhausted.

"You want to wait for everyone to get off, or do you want to be one of the first off?" he asked.

She was still sobbing, and he rubbed her arm. "Let's wait." Escorting a sobbing Zoe from the plane would raise eyebrows, and Dobby warned him they would have a welcoming party. He hadn't mentioned that to Zoe yet.

As people started disembarking, Zoe sat up and he handed her a clean napkin.

"Sorry." She dabbed her eyes.

"No need to be. I'm feeling pretty emotional to be home myself." He gave her a minute to get hold of herself and then said, "A few people will be waiting for us when we get out."

"Not just my parents?"

"No." Though he had insisted they be there. "Stefan and my boss want an immediate debrief."

She screwed up her nose and then sighed. "Where are we going?"

"Don't know yet."

"Do we need to get our story straight?" she asked.

Heath shook his head, ridiculously touched that she would even think of lying for him. "You tell the truth," he said. "Though maybe don't mention the kissing."

She smiled. "All right."

When the aisles finally cleared enough, Heath stood and waited for Zoe to precede him as they left the plane. It was late afternoon and the sun blazed through the windows of the gate, a dry heat that immediately felt welcoming. He inhaled deeply. It smelled like home.

At the end of the walkway he spotted Dobby and Major Hammond. The major looked unimpressed. That was his usual expression, but Heath noticed his eyes narrow as Heath placed his hand on Zoe's back to allow her to go through the door first.

Yep, he had some explaining to do.

Next to the men was Stefan with a purple suitcase he suspected belonged to Zoe, and beside him were a man and a woman. The female's resemblance to Zoe was uncanny.

Zoe gasped and ran the remaining distance to her parents. She flung her arms around them, and they surrounded her in a hug.

Heath's heart broke a little for her. It wouldn't be easy to reconcile everything she had seen, but he would be there for her if she still wanted him to be.

He stopped in front of the Major and saluted.

"At ease," Major Hammond said. He glanced at Zoe as if annoyed by the emotion shown. "Let's go." He turned and walked away.

Heath glanced at Dobby and then at Zoe.

"Debrief back at base," Dobby said, and then lowered his voice. "Major came to make sure there were no delays in you getting there."

Right.

Zoe separated from her parents, and before Heath could speak, Zoe's mum hugged him. "Thank you for getting my baby home safely."

Heath hugged her back, his heart filling. This

was why he did what he did. To keep families together and safe. "Zoe barely needed my help."

When she clung a little longer than was necessary, her husband put a hand on her back. "My turn." He grinned at Heath and when she stepped back, he grabbed Heath in a manly hug. "Thank you."

"You're welcome," Heath responded, touched by the affection.

Stefan cleared his throat, and Heath glanced at him. "Zoe, we need to do our own debrief."

She nodded.

"I'll call you," Heath said. "Make sure you're settling in OK."

She smiled. "Thank you."

Every fibre in him screamed for him to hug her and not walk away, but he had to.

At least she was safe now. What came next for them was anyone's guess.

***

When Heath walked out of the debrief with Dobby, it was already dark. The Major had gone over every detail to make sure there was nothing that could get back to them politically and cause an international incident. It turned out that Lotfi had been taken in for questioning and they'd found Zoe's phone on him. After a short session with the UAE tech people, they'd found the deleted photo of the witch.

The witch was now at the highest security prison and awaiting trial.

Zoe and Heath had been cleared of any wrong-doing.

There wasn't much chatter yet about the Iranian navy vessel, but Iran was probably keen to keep that quiet, assuming smugglers had been able to overwhelm one of their boats, which was never a good look.

"You want a beer?" Dobby asked.

He wanted to see Zoe, but she would be catching up with family, and he didn't have her number because her phone was still in the UAE. But Dobby would have her number. "Yeah."

"The rest of the guys want to hear what happened," Dobby added.

"Whose place?"

"Yours?"

Heath nodded. It would be good to chat about what had happened without needing to watch his words, and his teammates would be curious.

Dobby made a call and all he said was, "Joker's place."

Heath grinned as he got into his car. He loved his friends. Word would get around and some of them might beat him home. "See you there."

It felt a little surreal to drive out on the streets of Perth. It always was after a mission where he was constantly alert for danger. Traffic wasn't too busy at this time of night and the drive was peaceful. He focused on his breathing, trying to disconnect from being mission-ready.

People went about their everyday lives and didn't have to worry about bombs or guns.

Safe. Secure.

That veneer was broken for Zoe. She'd seen the other side and she wouldn't be able to fully go back.

He would help her however he could.

Fifteen minutes later he pulled into his garage and spotted Rhys's car out front. He grinned. Always the first to a party.

He waved and unlocked the front door as Rhys crossed the lawn, looking every bit the preppy white boy.

"Glad you're in one piece." Rhys hugged him.

"Me too." He flicked on some lights and headed for the kitchen as Dobby and then Noah came in carrying a few pizzas. "Mitch?" Their last teammate wasn't a regular at their social catch-ups because his wife was eight months pregnant and didn't like him to go far.

Heath had seen the stress on his face when they'd flown to Qatar. The relationship had been a little turbulent before she'd become pregnant, and now it was one spark from an explosion.

Noah shook his head.

Shame, but Heath would catch up with him later. "Romeo?"

Noah sniggered. "Hot date."

Heath grinned. Romeo was still new to the SAS and enjoying the perks that came with the title.

He passed out beers, and they settled on his comfortable sofa and opened the pizza boxes. The smell hit him, and he inhaled deeply. The airline food hadn't been great. He grabbed a slice and savoured the taste.

"So what the hell went wrong?" Rhys asked.

He swallowed and laughed. "It would be a shorter story if I told you what went right." And then he launched into the tale, being careful to avoid mentioning how close he and Zoe had become. His teammates wouldn't judge him, but he wanted to keep it to himself.

When he was finished, Dobby said, "So you and Zoe a thing?"

Heath laughed. Why had he thought he could keep it a secret from his closest friends? "What makes you say that?"

"The way your gaze barely left her at the airport, the promise to call her later." Dobby handed him a piece of paper. "That's her parents' number by the way."

This was why he would do anything for these men. "Thanks." He smiled. "She's pretty special. She fought for those kids even when she had no idea how to get them off the ship."

"What did the Major say?" Noah asked.

"Suspension pending further investigation."

"You don't seem too cut up about it," Rhys said.

He glanced at Dobby. "Actually I was going to ask Dobby about his security firm."

"Shit, don't tell me we're going to lose you too," Noah said.

"There are a lot of kids getting smuggled, lots of people needing help out there."

"And none who can afford to pay," Rhys pointed out. "How will you earn a living?"

"There would be clients who could afford to pay well." Heath looked at Dobby. "Where are you with that?"

"It's coming together, but to buy the equipment we require, we're going to need an investor."

Heath grinned. "About that. I happen to know where you can find a few million."

***

Zoe was unemployed. It really wasn't unexpected, but she was surprised by Stefan's insistence on telling her immediately. He'd taken her to a room at the airport, not unlike the one Lotfi had locked them in, so she could tell him what had happened, but she was sure he'd already made his decision. Stefan was just tidying up this matter before he caught a plane to Canberra later that night.

She skimmed the details, saying they had time during the dust storm to look into the children's whereabouts and that the ship had set sail earlier than they'd expected.

She didn't go into detail about what had happened on the navy boat or at Dubai airport. He already knew what the military was willing to tell him.

Finally he accompanied her into the public area where her parents were waiting for her in a coffee shop.

Stefan stuck out his hand. "Good luck, Zoe."

Zoe shook his hand in response. He didn't care if she succeeded or not. Her actions had become a blot on his record, proof he couldn't control his staff, and he wasn't pleased by it.

After he left, Zoe hugged her parents again. "Let's go home."

Her father drove, and she stared out the window at the orderly traffic and familiar buildings.

So normal.

So safe.

The sun was setting as her father pulled into the drive. As he got her suitcase out of the boot, her mother said, "Your sisters want to see you, if you're feeling up for it."

"Sure." Zoe had rested enough on the plane and she didn't want to repeat the story too many more times.

"How about we get fish and chips for everyone?" her dad suggested.

Zoe nodded. "That sounds great."

She followed them into the house, which had barely changed since her childhood. Maybe a fresh coat of paint of a different colour, but the layout and decorations were the same. She smiled as the tension in her shoulders released.

"You can sleep in your old room," her mum said.

Zoe followed her father into the bedroom. This had changed. Gone were the posters of her youth and her single bed, and in their place was a photo of a Highland cow on the wall and a double bed and dresser.

Still it was comforting.

Her dad left the suitcase by the dresser. "Why don't you freshen up while we invite the others and organise dinner?"

"Thanks, Dad." She kissed his cheek, and he hugged her.

"Just glad you're safe."

Zoe turned away so he wouldn't see the tears well in her eyes, and busied herself unzipping her suitcase, which she'd packed when word got out that the embassy was leaving. She didn't have a lot of Western clothes in there. Just things she wore around her apartment. The rest were more appropriate for going out in public in Qatar.

She found a jumper and a loose pair of pants which would work and headed into the bathroom.

She sighed as she glanced at herself. She still had bags under her eyes and a heaviness that came with fatigue.

Tomorrow would be soon enough to think about her future. In the morning she'd research options, call Dobby to get Heath's phone number, and maybe he could put her in touch with the woman who'd helped them settle into Australia.

She could take any job in the meantime so she could find a place of her own. As much as she loved her parents, she couldn't imagine staying with them for too long.

She showered, changed, and by the time she returned to her room, she could hear her sisters in the living room.

Zoe braced herself and walked out as her

father came through the front door with a large wrapped parcel of fish and chips. Her mother had set the table with an array of condiments and some plates.

So incredibly normal, something they'd done so many times before.

And yet she felt apart from it, as if it was just a façade or a play she was watching from the outside.

She hugged her sisters and took a seat at the table, already knowing she wasn't going to tell them everything.

Knowing life couldn't go back to how it was.

She was no longer the same.

Chapter 18

Heath slept late the next morning. Even with his suspension, he would have to keep training, but as the mission had taken longer than expected, he had a day in lieu. When he finally got up, he made a coffee and then went to visit his mother. It was a Saturday, so she wouldn't be working, and he wanted to tell her about the witch.

She deserved some closure.

When he pulled up, she was in the front garden weeding. She straightened and smiled, stripping off her gardening gloves as he got out of the car.

"Heath, this is a lovely surprise."

"Hey, Mum." He pulled her into a hug, her small frame nestling into his. He tried to visit her a couple of times a month, but it wasn't always possible.

She patted his back and pulled away. "Is everything OK?"

"Let's go inside." He hadn't quite figured out how to broach the subject. They hadn't spoken about the witch in years. Perhaps his mother had dealt with the trauma, and bringing it up again would cause her further anguish.

"Is Leila OK?" she asked, worry on her face.

"As far as I know." He squeezed her hand as they walked inside. "I wanted to talk to you about something that happened on my latest mission."

She frowned at him as she went into the kitchen and pulled a jug of water out of the fridge. "Are you allowed to tell me?"

He nodded. "It relates to the night we left Iran."

His mother stilled, her gaze flashing to his, a hint of anguish on her face.

"I ran into the man who stopped us."

The blood drained from her face, and she rushed to him, rubbing his arms, checking for injuries. "He didn't hurt you?"

"No, Mum." He stilled her hands and said, "I hurt him."

Satisfaction filled her face. "Did you kill him?"

Heath shook his head. "But he's in gaol and will die for his actions."

She gasped. "The Dubai airport. You were there?"

He was impressed she'd made the connection. "I can't tell you that," he said. "But you don't have to worry about him hurting anyone else, ever again."

She squeezed him tightly, clinging for a moment longer than necessary. "Thank you." She stepped back, kissed his cheek, and poured their drinks. "It was the one thing I worried about over the years, even though I've dealt with what he did to us. I hated the thought of him out there, hurting others the same way he hurt our family."

She spoke so matter of fact about it.

"I never told you how much I admired your strength," Heath said.

She gave him a small smile. "We never spoke about it. You and your sister were so young. I tried to shield you from as much as I could."

"But I know what you went through, Mum. I can't comprehend how difficult it must have been for you to have gone through what you did, losing dad, being assaulted, and having two children to look after."

She nodded. "You always were my protector. I worried about you, still worry when you go on a mission, but I understand why you do what you do." She smiled. "How was it for you to see the man again?"

He sipped the water she handed him. "I froze," he admitted. "It was unexpected, and I flashed back to that night, and I couldn't tear my eyes away from him. If it wasn't for Zoe…" He broke off, not sure he should have mentioned her name. He cleared his throat. "She knew about him, and distracted me, managed to get my attention back."

"Someone you work with?" his mother asked.

He shook his head. "Someone who shouldn't have been there, but who had tried to protect some children."

His mother smiled. "Is she someone I might meet one day?"

He grinned at her prying. "I hope so." He finished his drink and placed the glass on the table. "I thought I might put her in touch with Aggie. She wants to help people."

"Of course. I'll send you her number."

It was one thing he loved about his mother. She knew he couldn't talk about his work, and she respected that, content with what he could tell her.

"You should tell Leila about the man," his mother said.

He nodded. "I'll video call her later." They had spoken about that night once before, just before she'd flown to the United Kingdom. While she'd never seen the man—he'd sheltered her from that—she had seen their father get shot and knew something awful had happened to their mother.

Leila had told him she hoped all the men had

got what they deserved, but she would do her best to stop others like them.

"Now," his mother said, getting some biscuits out of the cupboard. "Why don't you tell me more about this Zoe who has put a gleam in your eye?"

He smiled and sat at the kitchen table as she placed the food on the table. "She's pretty incredible."

***

Zoe wasn't sure how early she could call Dobby for Heath's number. Would it seem too eager if she called before nine?

Would he even be available? They might still be debriefing, or back in training, or doing who knew what kind of special forces stuff.

So instead of calling, she spent the morning researching job opportunities, keeping the search broad to see what options she had available to her.

She also looked into one-bedroom apartments available in the area. Prices were astronomical, but she had some savings, and if she could find a job, she should be able to afford something near her parents.

Without her phone she couldn't call Nisha as she no longer had her phone number, but perhaps Heath could help her track it down.

The house phone rang and she glanced over to the landline that sat on the counter. Her parents still had one, despite almost always using their mobiles. Her mother dashed in to answer it, smiling at Zoe. "Hello?" She glanced at Zoe and grinned. "Heath, it's so lovely for you to call and check on her."

Zoe's heart jumped and she got to her feet.

"Of course. She's right here. She's spent all morning looking for work. You know they fired her because she wanted to rescue those poor children."

Zoe bit down on her impatience as Heath responded to her mother.

"Yes, it's ridiculous, but she's planning to stay in Perth, which we're so pleased about. We missed her."

She clenched her teeth together and resisted the urge to hold out her hand for the phone. Her mother loved a good chat.

"All right. You must come over for dinner soon," her mother said. "I'll get Zoe for you." Her mother handed over the phone with a cheeky glint in her eye.

She'd known exactly what she was doing.

"Hello."

"Hey, Zoe. How are you feeling today?"

She turned her back on her mother and closed her eyes as Heath's warm voice washed over her. Her chest ached. He was the only one who really understood what she'd been through. "Not bad. Still getting my head around everything."

"Yeah, it'll take some time. I've got the number of a good therapist and also Mum's friend, Aggie, for you."

"Thanks." What she really wanted was to see him again, to hold his hand or hug him.

"You free this afternoon?" Heath asked. "I thought maybe we could have that date we talked about."

Her heart leapt. "Sounds great."

"I'll pick you up in an hour." He hung up before she could ask him where they were going.

Zoe hung up and turned to find her mother grinning at her. "He's a nice man."

Zoe flushed. "Yes, he is. He's picking me up in an hour."

"Have fun, dear."

An hour later, Heath pulled into the driveway driving a white ute. "Bye, Mum." Zoe rushed out to meet him, not wanting her parents to detain them.

Heath raised his eyebrows as she slid into the passenger seat. "Hey."

"Hey." She let out a breath and smiled at him. "If you came in, it would be another hour before we left," she explained. "Mum and Dad want to hear your side of the story because they know I didn't tell them everything."

He nodded. "You have to fill me in on what they know." He backed out of the driveway. "You look good."

She'd found a summer dress one of her sisters had left at their parents' place and borrowed it. "Thanks. So do you."

He wore a navy blue T-shirt that hugged his muscles and a pair of shorts. Very casual.

"Where are we going?"

"Your choice," he said. "I packed a picnic, so we could head to the beach, or a park, or anywhere you like."

He remembered what she'd said about crowds.

It was Saturday and the weather was beautiful. The beaches and parks would be full of people enjoying the last glorious days of warmth before winter.

"Could we go to your place?" she asked. "Assuming you don't have any roommates who might be annoyed."

"No roommates," Heath said as he turned left onto the main road. "How are you really holding up?" He glanced at her with an expression full of concern.

She thought about it. "I'm OK, but it feels

surreal to be looking for work and an apartment a day after fleeing country after country, not knowing when we'd truly be safe."

He handed her a piece of paper. "The numbers I told you about. Aggie is the woman at the refugee centre who helped us when we arrived in Australia."

Zoe stared at the numbers and then tucked them into her bag. "Thank you."

"The therapist has security clearance so you can tell them everything you need to," Heath continued.

"Anything I shouldn't mention?"

Heath shook his head as he turned down a street not far from her parents' house. "You tell them everything you need to, Zoe. I want you to heal from this, and keeping things inside won't help."

"I don't want you to get into trouble," she said.

He shrugged. "I'm suspended pending further investigation," he said. "The army doesn't like it when a soldier goes rogue, but I wouldn't change a thing. Those kids needed to be saved."

"Have you heard anything more from Rambo?" Zoe asked.

Heath grinned. "The kids were returned to their families this morning," he said. "Nisha sent us a message via Rambo. I'll show it to you when we get inside." He pulled into the driveway of a dark brick house, probably built in the seventies. The front lawn was mowed and had a couple of garden beds in it with native plants. The garage door opened and the sides were lined with shelves with camping gear and power tools.

Zoe smiled. This is what she wanted. A glimpse into who Heath was when not on the job.

As Zoe got out of the car, the garage door descended, and Heath walked over to a door which led into the house, carrying a picnic basket.

She followed him down a short corridor to an open living area with a comfortable couch, photos of his team and two women that she assumed were his mother and sister, and a massive television. The kitchen bench had a couple of stools next to it, and Heath placed the hamper on the round table.

Zoe hesitated, a little uncertain now they were alone. All she wanted was to hug him, but it felt like such a long time since their conversation in the airport.

Heath turned to her and held his arms wide.

With a half sob, she threw herself into them and hugged him fiercely.

"You're safe now, Zoe. No one's going to hurt

you here."

She knew that, but her emotions were all over the place. As she drew comfort from his arms and his masculine scent, she glanced at him. "How are you? Any news on the witch?"

"He's in gaol," Heath said. "He'll be facing the firing squad."

Good. He'd no longer be able to hurt anyone. "Have you told your mother?"

"Yeah, I visited her this morning and called my sister before I picked you up. They're both relieved."

Zoe couldn't imagine what it must be like for them. With a sigh, she stepped back and cupped his face. "I'm glad you were able to stop him."

He smiled, pressing his cheek into her hand. "You stopped me from doing something rash at the airport. I'm not sure what I would have done if you hadn't distracted me."

Her gaze went to his lips. Their first kiss. His lips quirked upwards, and she looked him in the eyes. His expression was intense, and a spear of lust went through her.

There was no danger here.

Nothing they had to flee from. They had all the time in the world. She was no longer Heath's mission. "Can I kiss—"

"Yes," Heath cut her off. "Please."

She grinned and didn't know who moved first, but their lips met and finally she was kissing him the way she'd been wanting to.

His mouth plundered hers, and she moaned, pressing closer to him, feeling the heat radiating off his body.

Her fingers dug into his hair, and his groan of satisfaction sent more pulses of lust right to her core.

Everything about this man made her want him.

She broke the kiss and ran her hands down his chest, itching to get under his shirt. "Would it be too forward of me to ask where your bedroom is?"

The lust cleared from his gaze for a second as he asked, "Are you sure?"

"Yes." This wasn't a reaction to the circumstances they'd survived together. This was need for him; the incredible, sexy, kind man she wanted.

His expression turned slightly wicked and he lifted her as if she weighed nothing. "It's this way." She wrapped her legs around his waist and felt his desire as he carried her down the corridor to a bedroom that contained a very large bed.

He kissed her again and she clung to him until her need to touch grew too strong. She unlocked her legs and stood, her hands going straight to the bottom of his T-shirt and slipping under it.

His groan of appreciation lit up her insides as she ran her fingertips up over his hard muscles.

He shucked off the shirt and she gasped as she spotted the faint bruises on his torso.

"Doesn't hurt," he said as he dragged her closer again. Then his hands were sweeping up the bottom of her dress and cupping her butt, and her concern faded as her desire spiked again.

He pulled her against him and plundered her mouth, and Zoe became a boneless mess of need. She fumbled with the button on his shorts, and he slid the zip of her dress down, stepping back only long enough for it to fall to the floor, leaving her in her underwear.

His appreciative gaze scanned her body as she finally managed to undo his shorts and they joined her dress on the floor.

And oh my, he was definitely as turned on as she was.

Before she could blink, her bra was off and his mouth was on her breasts, kissing and sucking them as she threw her head back and moaned.

"You are beautiful, darling," Heath murmured. "I need all of you."

He lowered her to the bed and kissed his way down her body, spending time on each breast until she was writhing beneath him. "More," she begged.

His tongue licked a path down her stomach until he reached the waistband of her underwear.

She lifted her hips so he could take them off, but he pressed his mouth to her mound and licked.

Zoe gasped, the need so heavy in her. "Heath, please."

He ripped her underwear down her legs and then his mouth was on her and the sound that came out of her mouth was nothing short of feral.

He grinned as he slid two fingers inside her. "Zoe, darling, you are fucking incredible." He licked her clitoris and she whimpered as he moved his fingers inside her. She couldn't find words, couldn't tell him that she wanted him inside of her, could only ride the pleasure he was giving her.

"That's it, beautiful. Come for me. I can feel you clenching."

His words sent another pulse of lust through her, and the orgasm ripped through her. Her body bucked as he held her in position and continued to pleasure her.

Finally she sighed and he slowed, kissing his way back up her body and gently caressing her breasts. "You are amazing."

She still couldn't quite speak, but her hands slid to his crotch where he was still wearing underwear, but his cock was straining against the fabric.

"You want more, darling?" he asked with a cocky smile.

"Yes." She wanted to be one with him, and the enormity of the emotion was slightly scary. "Do you have condoms?"

He kissed her again, long and deep before reaching over and getting one from his bedside table.

Then he proceeded to slowly nibble and lick her breasts again. She squirmed. "Heath, I want you. Inside me. Now."

"Now don't be so impatient, love," he said. "I want you just as needy before I thrust into you for the first time."

She wasn't sure she would be able to handle it.

But true to his word, it wasn't long before she was hot and needy and begging him again.

He slid his underpants off and the condom on, settling his amazing body above her. She lifted her hips to accommodate him, and he kissed her deep, almost like a promise as he slid inside her.

Their groans intermingled as he moved, slowly at first, savouring the sensation.

Zoe had never had a lover with so much intensity mixed with kindness before.

She stared into his face as their movements increased, and she wrapped her legs around his waist, urging him on.

This time when her orgasm hit, his did too, and Zoe knew she wanted this man in her life forever.

Chapter 19

It took a long moment before Heath's heartbeat went back to normal. Zoe was incredible, and the way she snuggled into him after they'd cleaned up sent happy feelings flooding through his body.

He didn't want to let go.

Ever.

But it was too soon for such announcements. She was still dealing with everything that had happened to her. He kissed her forehead, and she stretched lazily.

"That was amazing," she declared.

"You're amazing," he countered. He hadn't been planning on getting her into his bed so quickly. He had a whole picnic planned, some time to talk, to get to know each other better. Though how a person reacted in a crisis told him a lot about them, and Zoe had reacted admirably.

He hesitated, not quite sure what to say.

Zoe kissed his cheek and shuffled onto her

elbow to look at him. "I feel like I should apologise."

He frowned. "Why?"

"You had this lovely picnic organised, and I jumped your bones before we could have any of it. It wasn't my plan when I asked to come here," she admitted. "I just wanted to be alone with you."

Heath chuckled as his heart warmed at her phrasing and confession. "I have no complaints," he said. "Jump my bones any time you want." He kissed her again because he couldn't help himself and sat up. "If you're hungry, I can bring the picnic in here."

Her eyes widened. "In bed?"

"Sure."

Her grin made his heart sing. "All right."

"Be right back." He brought up Rambo's video of Nisha on his phone and handed it to Zoe before striding out of the room. He placed a hand on his heart which felt like it had swelled to twice its size. He definitely had it bad for her.

He collected the basket and returned to his bedroom where Zoe was sitting up with the sheet pulled up over her breasts.

Shame.

She glanced at him, her eyes damp with tears. "They're all safe, thanks to you"

He smiled. "Thanks to us. You did as much

work as I did."

She brushed away the tears and nodded. "Us."

He liked the way that sounded. Quickly he spread the picnic blanket over the cover and pulled out the food he'd brought. He'd decided to go with fresh bread, cheeses, dips and more finger food, with a bit of barbecued chicken in case she wanted some meat.

"This looks incredible." She helped herself to the cheese and biscuits. She glanced at him. "I managed to eat some fish last night."

He smiled. "That's great." He settled next to her and helped himself to some baguette with pâté. "You might like to talk to Dobby's partner, Mila. We rescued her late last year. She had a different experience, but she'll understand a little."

"That would be great," Zoe said. "I'll call Aggie and the therapist on Monday as well."

He squeezed her hand. "Good. It will get easier, and I'm always here if you want to talk about it."

She stared at him, her expression serious, and he saw the same hesitation in her eyes as he had when she'd been debating about asking him about the kiss in the airport. "What is it?"

Zoe sighed with a smile. "You always seem to know what's going on in my head."

"You're an open book, darling."

She screwed her nose up and then blurted, "I really like you, Heath. Is that crazy considering we've only known each other a few days?"

"It's been an emotional experience," he said carefully. Her face fell, and he hurried to continue. "We've seen each other react in a heightened situation, and that brings a bond that we will never lose. But I really like you too. I want to spend time with you. I want to get to know who Zoe is when she's not running from bad guys, and I want to help you find what's next for you." He paused. "If you want me to."

"I'd like that." Zoe smiled.

He leaned over and kissed her. "Then we're in agreement. So why don't I warn… sorry, tell you about my teammates who all really want to meet you?"

Zoe grinned, though some concern crossed her features. "I can't wait to meet them."

He handed her another biscuit with cheese. "Settle in. This might take a while."

Continue the Series

Have you read Book 1 – Rescuing Mila yet?

Trapped on a shattered island after a tsunami, a special ops soldier and the woman he swore to protect must survive the elements — and the enemies still hunting her.

The next Squadron 6 book will be Rhys's (aka Axle's) story.

However if you want to discover what the team are like when they're not on a mission, make sure you check out the Lilydale Cottage series, starting with Book 1 – Repairing Dreams.

Acknowledgements

First of all I'd like to acknowledge the timing around publishing this book. When I wrote Protecting Zoe the USA had not yet attacked Iran, and the Strait of Hormuz was still open to shipping. Let's just say this book was set before then.

I did a lot of research about the Middle East trying to decide which country to set the book in. I knew from the outset I wanted Heath to face the trauma from his childhood, so it had to be near Iran.

I also learned a lot about cargo ships, dust storms and elevators!

I really enjoyed writing Protecting Zoe and I knew I'd got the action right when my editor, Ann Harth, told me she'd worked through several break sessions because she couldn't stop reading. Thanks Ann!

I also want to thank my copyeditor, Teena Raffa-Mulligan and cover designer, Megan from EmCat Designs for turning around the edits and print cover super fast so I could have print copies available for the Wild Out West book signing. You're both amazing.